I AWOKE TO TERROR

Something lean and dark was huddled on my windowsill. It put me in mind of a gigantic black jungle cat hunched and ready to spring. Even the claws—or one claw—sparkled in the light. It was a knife of some kind, long and surprisingly slender.

My body felt terribly cold and stiff. Even if I tried, I could not move fast enough to avoid that knife. There were only seconds left to me. I shook off my paralysis and, just as my deadly enemy leaped, sprang out of bed shrieking like a banshee. . . .

More Gothics from SIGNET

The Rest Is Silence

by Virginia Coffman

A SIGNET BOOK

NEW AMERICAN LIBRARY

TIMES MIRROR

SIGNET TRADEMARK REG. U.S. PAT. OFF. AND FOREIGN COUNTRIES
REGISTERED TRADEMARK—MARCA REGISTRADA
HECHO EN CHICAGO, U.S.A.

SIGNET, SIGNET CLASSICS, MENTOR, PLUME AND MERIDIAN BOOKS
are published by The New American Library, Inc.,
1301 Avenue of the Americas, New York, New York 10019

FIRST SIGNET PRINTING, OCTOBER, 1976

1 2 3 4 5 6 7 8 9

PRINTED IN THE UNITED STATES OF AMERICA

Chapter One

THE FLAT BUZZ of the bedside phone hung on the damp air of the little Richmond Hill hotel room, and I turned my head on the pillow, fumbling in the darkness for the phone, wondering for a minute where I was.

The first singsong accents of the desk clerk coming over the line caught my sleepy mind by surprise, and I thought: *A foreigner!* mentally hammering in the last Irish-oriented nail, *And English, at that!*

"Good morning, madam. Six-thirty," said the voice.

Glory be! I thought. *I forgot. It's their country. I'm the foreigner.*

I thanked the cheerful voice and hung up. And so I began my preparations for a grand show I was destined never to see, on a day that dropped me into an eerie world of silence and terror.

Shivering in the dawn of this momentous April day, I pulled the frayed cord of the bed lamp and felt for my travel slippers. I then did exactly what five or six million other dwellers of London and Surrey were doing at that minute. I hurried to the window, pushed aside the drapes, and peered out anxiously at the sky. Already, the usual weather of an English spring was well in evidence—drizzly fog, with a hint behind it of worse to come.

This disappointment was softened by my lowering glance, which took in the fairyland of red-white-and-blue buntings, flags, and standards that turned the little Richmond inns across the road into a setting worthy of the Tudor realm they imitated. No window was without its adornment of triangular pennants and large pictures of the Queen and the Duke of Edin-

5

burgh, carefully cut out of the Sunday pictorials and mounted on cardboard above the pictures of the Royal Wedding's young pair. It was as though the Queen, and not merely one of her close relatives, were marrying.

I felt the iciness of the weather outside seeping through the window glass against my cheek. I glanced once more at the darker smudges in the sky overhead and turned away to dress, realizing that the coming storm made it impossible to wear the terribly expensive Italian knit suit I had bought just before leaving home. I would wear my wool travel dress and perk it up with a Kelly-green kerchief bought in my native Los Angeles, where the sun was a mortal enemy to such greenness as I saw from this window. I had had to enforce rigid economies upon myself for fifteen months in order to invest in my solitary Grand Tour of Europe, against all the arguments of my father and mother, who had fled from the Dublin of the Troubles in 1921 and couldn't imagine any daughter of theirs spending her hard-earned money to go visiting "the enemy."

Still and all, Mother got quite a thrill when it looked as if I'd see a Royal Wedding, even if it was in the country of Pa's hated Black-and-Tans, and my parents' bon voyage present had been a wonderful fifty-dollar ticket to the grandstands in London so that I could see the Procession on its way to Westminister Abbey and then again on its return. And there'd be uniforms and music, and a grand box lunch with all manner of delicious things—salmon pasties, Bambury cakes, raisin scones with butter, coffee, tea, and a dozen other mouthwatering delicacies. Then, there was the television in the stands as well, so we could see the fine show, the costumes and the bride's great train, and the ceremony in the Abbey itself. How could Pa say it was all "blather" and not worth fifty dollars? And anyway, he gave Mother the money to buy the ticket for me.

As I dressed before the dim, quaint mirror of the dresser, I felt quickly for my ticket. I studied the huge

yellow pasteboard, handling it as if it were gold-plated
—as, indeed, it was to a household that was no richer
than us O'Cartys. It had my very own name on it, as
well:

ADMIT MISS NONA O'CARTY
TO SEAT NO. 15, ROW U,
BLOCK B, STAIRCASE NO. 3.

And then there was a great deal of tiny print, and
on the back was a clear map showing the position of
the stands near Westminster Abbey.

Everything depended upon this wonderful yellow
pasteboard so large that it wouldn't fit into my small
clutch purse. My grandstand ticket and my passport
were both too big for this silly purse. When I had finished dressing, I hid my passport in one of my nylon
slips and shoved it to the back of the dresser drawer.

Dressed now for the English weather, I had no false
pride at sitting amid the mink-and-sable overseas visitors in my old black wool coat with its warm standing
collar. With the deftness of long practice I tied over
my head and under my chin a twin of the green scarf
I was wearing at the throat of my dress.

"Now, you're a peasant and no mistake," I told my
reflection.

Picking up my purse and the precious yellow ticket,
I went downstairs through dark, wood-paneled byways
of the inn to the promised early breakfast. The desk
clerk looked up as I rounded the newel post on the
lower floor and started through the American Bar,
which had been crowded last night but was now
gloomy and forsaken in the gray morning. Beyond the
bar I could hear a buzz that suggested that other Royal
Wedding visitors were already in the dining room.

Once in the dining room, I found myself among a
conglomeration of confident fellow-American voices en-
livened now and then by the up-the-scale tones of the
English waitress. As usual at breakfast, there was no

menu. All Englishmen knew that Americans ate fried eggs, two slices of cold toast, and two strips of under-done bacon every day and were finicky about the thickish brown liquid they referred to nostalgically as "American-style coffee." This breakfast stared me in the face now. With a memory of certain utilitarian little cafés back home, I thought, *Oh, for a glass of orange juice and a plain little doughnut!*

Seeing the reproachful eyes of the waitress on me, I nibbled around the edge of the gelid fried egg, doc-toring it up with pepper and salt; but, like the dinners I had eaten in the otherwise charming little hotel, it had all the full, rich flavor of fried English woolens. I sus-pected that the brave English never noticed the differ-ence.

Surrendering the bacon, which I couldn't quite cut, I took up the toast, but it sent a clammy chill through my fingers, and I put it down hastily and broke it up so that the waitress would think I had eaten some of it.

It was now seven-ten, and I wasn't sure just how mobbed the underground would be as it tried to accom-modate what must surely be one of the largest crowds since the Coronation.

"Grand show!" said the blue-eyed waitress, beaming in her friendly way. "Fair gives you the shivers think-ing of it. They say the bride's gown is magnificent. You'll be taking a program, Miss?"

A program. I had forgotten that. Many of Europe's last remaining royalty would pass, and great folks of the Commonwealth, and I wouldn't know one prince-ling from another.

"Never mind, Miss. You can get a lovely one at Richmond Station. Only two and six. You'll see. Why, here you've gone and forgot your seat cheque, ma'am. That'll never do."

"I'll forget my head next, I thought as I snatched up the yellow pasteboard, thanked the girl, and hurried out to the little foyer of the hotel. An ancient taxi,

piloted by a driver with a fiery red handlebar mustache, was waiting, and I got in.

The taxi bumped down the hill under decorations streaming in the wind and not the least subdued by the night's dampness. The streets were surprisingly deserted. Apparently everyone was already in London. All the shops lining the street were closed, so it would be necessary to get the program when I bought my underground ticket, and that meant bucking the crowded stairways. Three cabs had already pulled up in front of the weathered old station, and as my own driver showed an anxiety to get back to the next haul, I asked him to stop half a block this side of the station and let me out.

I found myself on the wet and almost empty sidewalk of this quaint little foreign town, surrounded by hostile, closely barred shops, and felt a desolate loneliness for my family. Suddenly, for no reason except the piercing dampness, I would have given anything to be safely back at my desk in a Hollywood office where there would be nothing to think about, no excitement, no homesickness, only the big problem—would I be kept overtime tonight, or could I get out in time to go and see the European travelogue at the Cinerama Theatre.

I walked a few steps, hugging my purse and the yellow ticket to my breast, trying to restore circulation to my chilled body. I noticed then that the door of a small stationer's store across the street was ajar. I could see the day's newspapers, their front pages alive with stunning portraits of the Queen as well as the royal bride and groom, carelessly flung along a counter just inside the door. Surely, the shopkeeper would also sell programs.

I ran across the street and pushed open the door. Inside, the store was dark. Whatever stationery and books the little room carried were covered by grimy strips of old newspapers. There was a door at the rear, leading into the living quarters or perhaps a storeroom.

I coughed, then cleared my throat. No one came. On the counter by the door were bundles of the *Times*, a Sunday pictorial, and a scattering of other metropolitan dailies. Something under the *Times* glistened like gilt paper, and I pulled it out. It was one of the Approved Souvenir Programmes with its gold insignia of the two royal families involved in the wedding. I set down my purse and yellow ticket, riffled through the booklet, and found that it was just what I wanted, giving the line of march and the identity of the groups participating. Still no one had appeared from the inner room. I glanced at my watch.

Seven-forty-five. I couldn't wait much longer.

"Is anybody here?"

By this time I half-expected to be answered by silence, but the handle of the inner door was turned as if by a cautious hand, and a sour-faced little man with a bent back stuck his head in. He seemed surprised to see me and scowled.

"What d'ye want? It's a paper ye're after? We're not open now. Holiday."

"It's just a wedding program. May I?"

"Two and six," said the old man automatically, looking behind and around me. "You come in alone? You see nobody else?"

"I am alone. Why?"

"No reason. Expectin' someun."

I looked into my purse, counted rapidly to myself among the confusing silver coins, and finally laid down what looked like a fifty-cent piece and was labeled "half-crown." Picking up my purse and program, I hurried out, my own lighter footsteps dogged by the squeaking shoes of the shopkeeper. He came to the doorway, peering intently up and down the drizzly street as I crossed to the station. I looked back once and saw that he had forgotten me already. Apparently I was not as important as his expected visitor.

I swung into the stream of low-murmuring commuters, wondering at this strange calm of the English, who neither pushed nor shoved nor glanced at their watches, yet gave every indication that they would reach their destinations at precisely the correct moment. As I waited to buy my underground ticket, two women behind me examined the previous night's paper and then glanced at me.

"American?" one woman asked the other in a whisper behind me.

I listened, curious.

"Irish, probably. Had a maid with a face like that—before the War, of course. Sweet, bright creature she was, too."

I wondered how that was meant and persuaded myself it was a compliment.

"Rather!" said the other woman, and changed the subject. "Jolly good weather for the show. No rain yet."

I ran down the steps and through the gate toward the train, feeling now the pent-up excitement of the great day to come. I seated myself where I could watch the stations map above the opposite seats, so I would know when I came to the correct interchange. What was the funny little street that would take me directly to the stands? It was in fine print at the bottom of my ticket.

I reached for the yellow pasteboard and found my lap empty! I opened my program and let the pages fly . . . I uselessly examined the too-small purse. The big yellow ticket was not there. Fifty dollars . . . a precious seat in the covered stands, the great box lunch that would give me dinners for several nights . . . I had lost it.

A quick glance told me at once that it wasn't on the train. A warning jolt somewhere . . . I had only an instant to get off. I sprang for the door just as it was closing, and jumped off the train. All along the passage and up the steps I moved slowly, my gaze combing every inch of the floor. Another line had formed at the train-ticket window. There was no yellow pasteboard at anyone's feet.

Breathless from my run up the steps, I went over to a friendly-looking bald man in station uniform.

"I beg your pardon. I've lost . . . I've lost . . ."

"Now, Miss, gently—gently does it. If you've lost it here, you'll find it right enough. Nobody here going to steal it, you know. What've you lost?"

"My ticket to the stands. A big yellow one. I must have dropped it."

He looked around from force of habit, but he was perfectly aware that I had already searched the station floor.

"All right now, Miss. Let's think back. You likely set it down somewhere."

"No. I came straight from my hotel to the station. I know I had it in my hand when I got in the taxi. And I had it in my hand when I stopped across the street at—"

Excitedly, I covered my mouth with my gloves hand. "That's it! I left it on that pile of papers in the little man's shop."

The station attendant beamed to see that British honesty had been vindicated.

"Now, you've got it. You run along and don't you be worrying. There'll be another train, quick as a wink. You'll get to London for the grand show, to be sure."

At the station entrance an elegant gentleman in a spandy-new bowler and cane glanced after me with that mixture of polite curiosity and puzzlement which seemed to say, "Life in the States must be hectic!"

It had not been ten minutes since I left the stationer's shop, but the door was now closed and the place looked deserted. Intimidated by its desolate look, I tried the door softly and, when it yielded, stepped inside, aware of my pulse beating heavily as I looked around for the big yellow ticket. If it were not here . . .

I saw it on the floor at the far end of the counter and tiptoed over to pick it up, hoping the old stationer would not catch me at it. He wasn't the friendliest soul in the world, and it would be better all around if he never knew I had returned.

Close to the rear door now, I became aware of the murmur of voices in the room beyond. As I stooped to pick up the ticket, the knob of the rear door was turned hard by a decisive hand. I stiffened against the counter with the fifty-dollar ticket safe in my fingers.

The door opened partway and remained open, held there by a man's hand and arm. I couldn't see the man, but his sleeve was heavy tweed, probably a topcoat.

". . . blackmail, my dear Putney, and there's the truth," said a clipped, decisive, North-of-England voice that went along with the arm. I ducked aside guiltily and wished I were out on the street, where my presence could not embarrass the unpleasant little shop owner or his forceful guest. The door opened a little wider, and from my dark corner I could see more clearly—and I didn't want to see this at all. I wanted only to get out without arousing these quarreling men.

A glaring, unfrosted light bulb dangled from the ceiling of the back room and illuminated all the harsh, surly, mean little lines in the shopkeeper's face as he hunched back against the open shelves behind him, where a six-month accumulation of old papers and rags was stacked. He had grinned at the word "blackmail," and the display of the uneven stubs of his yellow teeth, directed at the unseen man, changed his face from ugly to hideous. But in spite of his bravado, I noticed that his hands must be nervous, for he put them behind him. Was he leaning back upon them? They seemed to be buried among the dirty papers and rags of the shelf. His little eyes were fastened upon his visitor; yet when I moved, hoping to escape from this intolerable eavesdropping, his eyes shifted to the open door and I hesitated, trembling suddenly, feeling my hands and feet numb with cold. I would then be in the direct line of the shopkeeper's vision through the partially open doorway.

"Well, Putney, what do you say?" the unseen man's

voice resumed. "Why not be sensible now? Just betray them instead. It can't make any possible difference to you."

"No difference! Likely!" The shopkeeper's thin lip twisted in a way that must be habitual, for a heavy wrinkle had been carved there, running upward like a scar from the corner of his lip. "That's funny, that is. What've you got to offer me? They've hundred-pound notes. Match them and then we'll talk."

The unseen man's hand and sleeve dropped away from the doorknob, and he said pleasantly, almost humorously, "Putney, you really are of no use to anyone, are you? Now, let's consider—you must have an heir to this shop. A nephew, niece, cousin—yes. If I chose, I might make some heir very happy. I wonder who."

I could see the shopkeeper stiffen as I myself stiffened at the threat. The shopkeeper's eyes were hypnotized by the man who confronted him, and I realized that the shopkeeper looked as if he was in a killing mood. I had to get out of here, to call for help for one of them. I stood up as the shopkeeper's hands, busy behind him, suddenly pulled a long-barreled pistol out of the rags and aimed at his assailant. In the same instant there seemed to be an explosion in the back room, directed toward the shopkeeper. The shopkeeper stood there looking stupefied, his mouth falling open, his body going slack as he swayed. The pistol in the dying shopkeeper's hand missed its target, winking fire at the doorway. Turning to run, I felt a slap at the side of my head and heard first a roaring, like a waterfall, then —a long silence.

Chapter Two

I AWOKE without opening my eyes and wondered, within the painful, somnolent dark of a headache behind my eyelids, how soon it would be time to get up and go to work. Mother should be calling me very soon. It must be early still, because I couldn't hear a sound, and I generally was awakened by the fury of the diesel trucks, long-haul transfers, and fire engines that made up an everyday morning on a California freeway.

I opened my eyes and recognized the hotel room on Richmond Hill, strangely comforting in the unaccustomed sunlight that poured through the quaint squares of the window.

First I saw the faded bunting on the Tudor houses across the road, and then, far beyond the green hillside, the winding Thames, gleaming under the sun. How could that be? All the papers had predicted rain for the royal wedding. There was something else, small but inexplicable. A potted red geranium of the cheap, sturdy, easy-to-grow variety sat on the windowsill, and it certainly had not been there last night. Last night I had left a call for six-thirty this morning. What was wrong?

It must be past noon; the light seemed westerly. I would never be able to get to my seat in the stands. And would the underground be running during the actual procession? I sat up quickly and groaned as my head began to throb. There was a bandage stuck on above my left ear, and what was more disconcerting, my hair had been shaved in one place just behind my ear. Fortunately, the long hair tumbling from the top of my scalp would cover it.

Gradually, I remembered the shooting in the shop-keeper's back room and the queer slap against the side of my head. So it was not a dream. I had risen at the correct time, and afterward, the lost ticket . . . the little shop . . . I put my fingers up experimentally and groaned as I felt the tender spot. Or had I groaned? No sound shattered the singular quiet of the room. I cleared my throat, listening for the sound.

Silence.

I sat up again in panic and tried to concentrate on just what sounds did reach me. I was gradually aware of a low, roaring noise and the sound of something like wings beating in a cold, black cave. It filled my ears, blocking out every other sound. I called out, trying to control my voice at first, but it got away from me and I had no notion whether it was loud or soft, but I could not hear a syllable of it.

"Hello. Is anybody here? Hello! Hello!"

In panic, I thought, *What's the matter with my hearing? Nothing comes. . . . No sound . . .*

"Hello!" I said. "Where are you? Please come, some-body. . . . Please!"

I began to cry. Never in my life had I been so terri-fied. I had been taught to be self-reliant, to use my own devices when necessary, to enjoy being alone some-times. But not like this, cut off from all sound, in a strange room in an alien land. Where had the world of human beings gone?

In a gingerly way I put one foot out of bed, sur-prised at my weakness. It was all I could do to stand up, and I had to sit down immediately on the side of the bed before I could get the strength to search for my slippers. Feeling a faint, unfamiliar constriction around my waist, I looked down and saw that the fringed sash of my neat, boyish pajamas had been tied in a bow instead of a loose knot. Who had undressed me and got me into my nightclothes?

I caught sight of myself in the old mirror across the room and was shocked. Within a cloud of disheveled hair, my face had lost its healthy color. My eyes looked enormous. I couldn't stand my fears and uncertainties any longer and stood up, wavered, reached for a chair, and sat down suddenly with a bump that jarred my whole spine.

Then I thought of the telephone.

I fumbled for it, prayed that I would hear the sing-song English voice at the other end, but there was nothing. I spoke into the great, roaring silence. "Please send someone. . . . I think I'm sick," and hung up.

I hadn't the strength to get back into bed.

Time was confused. A long, long age later, and yet so short a time, I was startled and shrank away as two strong hands reached easily around my body, under my shoulders and knees, to lift me out of the chair. I made faint motions of protest, all of which were stifled against what seemed to be a white wall, but which beat comfortingly like a human heart.

Oh, he's the doctor, I thought drowsily. *I'll leave it all to him. . . .*

And I went to sleep.

The doctor was holding my hand now, and I was truly awake. It was very pleasant to absorb the strength of his fingers, so pleasant that I pretended to be asleep for a few seconds longer, just so I could watch him from under my lashes. I made out a dark, leonine head, a square face, saffron-hued and illuminated by expressive, deep-set dark eyes. But the effect of those eyes was almost counterbalanced by a mouth with thick-harsh lips that disturbed me in some indefinable way. I found the combination of the ugly mouth and the luminous eyes almost hypnotic. He had raised those eyes to my face now, and his hand moved toward my own eyes.

I became increasingly aware of my wretched looks —no lipstick, my hair uncombed, my cheap night-clothes wrinkled. I flushed in embarrassment, opening my eyes before he could touch me, and tried a smile to soften his bitter, sardonic expression. He looked as though he had very little sympathy for the world and none at all for himself.

I said, speaking carefully, hearing nothing, "I've been shot, haven't I?"

He reached past my cheek, his fingers exploring the bandage behind my ear. I felt the faint rubbing of the heel of his palm against my ear. It was a sensation almost unknown to me and strangely thrilling. As he bent over me, his eyes on my face, binding me to him by this invisible cord between the deaf and the speaker, I made out the words very easily on his harsh mouth.

"You are much better. You have been ill. You only came back from the nursing home last night."

"Nursing home? Me! I've never been sick a day in my life!" Then I remembered. "Oh. Because I was shot?"

"Not shot, Miss O'Carty. Shot *at*. It was a near miss, but it left a nasty bruise and knocked you out. I found you in the doorway of the Putney Shop." He had to repeat most of this, but it was surprisingly easy to follow his lips as he spoke.

"It was lucky you were passing. A doctor and all. I'm glad I didn't wake up in a . . . what you said. One of those nursing homes. They sound awfully depressing."

"It was a very nice nursing home, and you made such a fuss about it, I'm afraid we decided—that is, I decided—you would do much better to recover consciousness next time in your own familiar hotel room. The hotel has been most kind and cooperative."

"I made a fuss? I don't remember."

"You tossed and turned and grumbled. The police wanted you to remain there. But I insisted."

I stirred at this knowledge. "The police! Oh—because of my accident, you mean. I'd gone back for my ticket, you know. But he didn't mean to shoot me. He meant to shoot the other man. I should have known something would happen. It was such a gloomy morning. . . . The wedding! I missed the royal wedding!"

The faintest of smiles softened his face. "Oh yes. That was inevitable." I had the impression that he spoke with an accent, because he enunciated so clearly, accenting each syllable.

"Then you really are a doctor? That was lucky for me."

"My practice is in Richmond."

"I like your town—or I did like it before this happened. I liked London, too. I wanted so much to see . . ." No point in thinking of all I had missed, a sight perhaps never to be repeated in history.

He was watching me intently. It made me nervous, terribly aware of my shabbiness. *Next time I fall ill,* I thought, *I'll be wearing a sexy nightgown.*

"Have I been sick very long?"

I watched his lips for his answer.

"Three days. Traumatic shock. You remember nothing of that time? No matter. You are coming on well now."

I was alarmed and tried to sit up. His hands closed on my shoulders and forcibly restrained me. He was not ungentle, but there was too much power in his hands. I had not thought that doctors were so strong. It didn't seem normal.

"When will I hear again?"

He said something, and I asked him to repeat it. Even then I was surprised at what I made out. "That I am sure the police would like to know."

"The police! You mean because the man shot me? But I know he didn't mean to."

"Nevertheless, you must identify a picture of the man who fired at you. And tell whatever else you remember about that inner room, how much money you spent, who was there when you—"

"Money!" I felt a new panic. "Whatever happened to my money?"

"Would you like your purse?"

I was amazed when he reached around behind me and produced it from under my pillow. Like most of my property it looked shabby and dreadfully proper, an Irish working girl's black plastic handbag. While he watched me with his peculiar, sardonic look that almost revealed a sense of humor, I searched the bag. My traveler's checks were all there, four hundred dollars in twenty-dollar denominations for my tour of Continental Europe; then there was my tissue-thin return ticket, cabin-class, on the dear old *Queen Mary*. These worries, at least, were solved.

I looked up. I hardly dared to ask, "Will I always be deaf? Honestly, tell me the truth."

"My dear child, your hearing will return at any time. Perhaps any moment. There is no irreparable damage. You have had a shock. A near miss, that is all. The danger from the bullet. The other danger, of course, is another matter."

I didn't make out the exact words, but as he spoke, his black eyebrows went up like inverted V's and I understood them very well.

The overwhelming loss came over me then in a rush, like a sudden green wave foaming unexpectedly over my head, and I felt stifled, drowning. I covered my face with my hands. "If I don't get over it, I'll have to go home. And I'll never have the money to see Europe again."

He took my fingers from my face, removing each finger separately as if he found pleasure in this harsh, deliberate exertion of his strength upon me.

"Look at me!"

I understood that almost instinctively though I was not watching his lips. I raised my head slowly not caring that my face was blurry with tears.

"You may have your sightseeing trip. You are not permanently deaf, and you must stop thinking you are. You may regain your hearing in ten minutes. Or tonight. Or perhaps next week. Any time soon. These things are hard to predict. They depend upon the intangibles. But you must not agitate yourself. That will only delay your recovery. Now! The police will want to talk to you. Can you remember what happened that day in the Putney Shop?"

"Yes; yes, certainly. Mr. Putney started to fall, and the gun went off and hit me. I was in the shop by the door."

"He was not there alone?"

"Of course not. The man who shot him was there."

"Take your hands away from your face and look at me. So. I will not eat you. I am trying to make this as easy as possible for you. Tell me what you have to tell, and I will try and explain to the Scotland Yard men when they arrive. Who was this other man?"

"I don't know. I didn't see him."

The doctor nodded. "It's as well. You are in enough trouble without some gunman after you."

"But I heard him."

"Ah."

I expected him to say more, at the very least to admire my alertness, but he was listening for something. He seemed to have forgotten that he was still holding my hands in his. His fingers squeezed my fingers; then he thrust them from him with so much force that their fall made the bed jump. I was startled and tried to see behind him.

In the doorway was a tall, plump nurse with apple cheeks and very bright little round eyes. Peering over her shoulder were two nondescript men in loose overcoats with the general behavior of well-instructed tradesmen making a call on the squire's wife. The doctor made a sweeping, un-English gesture toward me, said something to the two men, and got up from the bed. He stood back, exchanging a few words with the nurse, while the men moved up to my bed in a gingerly way. I felt like telling them that they needn't walk on tiptoe. I couldn't hear them if they pounded in with hobnailed boots. The two men looked rather alike without actually having similar features. It was their manner, their clothes, their lean, ruddy, Anglo-Saxon look, I supposed. The shorter man spoke first. He had unruly sandy hair and was rather good-looking—for an Englishman. I did not think his eyes looked like a detective's eyes at all. They were a friendly kind of blue.

He said something polite. It wasn't good morning, and it was muffled and spoken very quietly. For fear of disturbing a deaf woman? It was hard enough to understand English people in the best of circumstances, I thought, but this was going to be a real trial.

"Could you make your lips form the words more slowly?" I asked. "Like Doctor . . . like the doctor here."

Both men looked around at the doctor, who seemed pleased at my words. He stepped forward until he was at the foot of the bed. I had a sense of being penned in by the three men, like a baby in a crib, and I felt all the more uneasy.

The sandy-haired man said, with great care, "I am Detective Inspector MacLeish." He motioned toward his partner and gave some name that looked like "Framsby." I couldn't make it out. Then he continued with great care, "Would you please be good enough to tell us . . ." After that, whatever he said was all mixed up, and I got a headache trying to unscramble it. I closed my eyes and cut off the conversation. It was too much strain. Only seconds later I felt a cool, hard hand upon my forehead and another on the pulse at my wrist. The hard hand gently moved over my face to my mouth, and I opened my eyes to find a glass at my lips and the doctor's keen dark eyes looking down into mine.

"Drink."

I drank a little. Unlike English toast, the water was warm.

"Now, tell these gentlemen what you told me. You heard the voice of the man who killed the shopkeeper. Isn't it so?"

Then the ugly little man had died. I had seen murder done. I nodded.

The Scotland Yard men glanced at each other. They said something to the doctor, who spoke to me. "Was there anything about his voice that struck you . . ." He had forgotten and spoken too fast. He amended now and repeated, ". . . struck you as distinctive—different?"

I wanted to be helpful. They must think me a perfect fool, so helpless that only one person could communicate with me. I felt a growing desperation. What would I do when the doctor was not around? How would I make myself understood? I tried to answer the doctor's question by speaking directly to the two Scotland Yard men, so they would know I wasn't trying to snub them, especially the nice Inspector MacLeish.

"He had an odd way of talking. Some kind of brogue. Scottish, I think. Or Welsh, or a Channel Islander."

The two men sighed at that. I could tell by the way their shoulders dropped. It occurred to me then that Scotland and Wales and the Channel Islands provided quite a big area for a killer.

Inspector MacLeish asked the doctor something, and the doctor was about to relay this to me, when I remembered the other thing.

"I saw his hand and his arm on the doorknob."

"Excellent!" exclaimed the taller man approvingly.

"Yes," I went on. "I remember. There was a coat sleeve, an overcoat, a worn gray tweed, the kind we call English tweed in the United States."

The two men nudged the doctor. He spoke to me. "Do you recall any rings?" That was a hard word. He finally pointed to his own third finger, where there might have been a ring. No wedding ring, I thought irrelevantly, and answered him.

"No. Just a hand. I noticed the tweed coat more than the hand."

There were a couple of more questions, which I answered to the best of my ability, and the detectives went away, but I had a feeling that they were not nearly as inconsequential as they looked. In spite of my own predicament, I felt no desire to be in the shoes of the man with the tweed coat while those two lean, unhurried Scotland Yard men wandered amiably along in his footsteps.

"Well, Miss, shall we make you comfy?" asked the nurse, buslting around, puffing up the pillow, pulling out the bedsheets, shifting me about as if I were made of rags.

"But I can't stay here," I said to nobody in particular. It was easy to talk out loud to myself now. I could not hear my voice, so it didn't sound at all strange to me. "I can't afford to stay here. I must go."

"You'll go nowhere," said the doctor, coming back and bending over the bed. "You must rest now. You will feel much better when you wake up. You may even find your hearing is very much returned."

"I'm not sleepy. Yes, I am. Did you put something in the water I drank?"

"Go to sleep. I will tell you all about it when you wake up."

"Honestly? I'll hear just like new?"

"Perhaps better. It is all a matter of the nerves. You must remain calm. Learn to enjoy life. You are too serious, my dear girl. Let others worry about the inspector's problems."

"Am I really in danger from the man with the tweed coat?"

"Perhaps. Most certainly after your hearing is restored."

That almost shook me wide-awake. "What do you mean by that?"

He looked at me with as bland an expression as his face could provide. "But Miss O'Carty, you will then be a menace to the killer. Your testimony as to his voice may be deadly for him."

"And for me." I swallowed hard. "Am I being protected at all?"

"Certainly. Although you are in no great danger until your hearing is restored."

He was brutally frank. I didn't think very much of it. Nevertheless, because he did fascinate me, I closed one eye and asked, "Are you going to tell me your name?"

"Why should that be of any concern?" But he did not look forbidding as he added, "Maximillian Brandt. Go to sleep, and when you wake you may get up."

I closed both eyes. He rose from the bed, as I could tell by the pressure on the mattress. I kept my eyes closed and thought, *Is the doctor married? I'll be asking the nurse.*

I hoped I had said this to myself, and after a pause I was relieved that nothing happened. But then I felt a sharp pinch on my chin, and my eyes popped open in amazement.

"Look at me when I am talking to you!" the doctor's lips told me.

"Y-yes?"

He laughed. His disturbing mouth did not look nearly so cruel. "No. The doctor is not married. Now, go to sleep!"

Chapter Three

My HEARING did not return "in ten minutes," as Dr. Max Brandt had told me was possible, but I had been sufficiently frightened that I was almost relieved to find that in every respect but my hearing I felt as good as new by the next day. Knowing that my continued deafness might save my life was no doubt a motivating force in my difficulty. Everyone was exceedingly nice to me, and I discovered there really was a man from the police, or Scotland Yard, or wherever, whose job it was to see that the murderer in the tweed coat didn't kill me.

I was very careful not to let Papa or Mother know precisely what had happened to me—about my being temporarily deaf, I mean—because I knew they would hustle me home, even if Papa had to set foot on "dread English soil" to do it. But I wrote them about the shop and Mr. Putney and my being a witness and all, allowing for a bit of the Irish exaggeration thrown in. And to tell the truth, as long as I didn't really believe very much in the immediacy of that danger, I felt like a heroine.

For two days I wasn't allowed to leave the little hotel, which got to be a bit of a bore after I had examined every hole and corner in the old Tudor building and made myself a nuisance by twice blundering in upon the cooks chopping vegetables on old-fashioned breadboards and once startling a barman who had begun, behind the scenes, to tipple on ginger beer when he thought himself alone.

I said to Dr. Brandt at lunch two days after I'd come to consciousness, "I feel strong as a horse. Is it your idea for me to stay here, Doctor? What's to happen when I've run out of money? And me seeing no more of the world than the tip of my nose."

He smiled, and I was surprised that a man can smile and still look so strange, so unhappy. What deep thoughts he must have, like so many of these middle Europeans one saw now and then.

"There is not as much to the world as you may imagine, Nona." He had been sitting opposite me as I ate, though he ate nothing himself. He seemed to get a great deal of pleasure watching me eat, which was not flattering to me, I thought, and now when I said indignantly, "I'd prefer to find that out for myself, if you please," he changed the subject in what I considered a very rude way.

"For a young *Fraulein*, you have an extraordinary appetite."

I understood those words without a bit of trouble but decided not to humor him by getting angry, especially since his nurse, the blond lady named Bertha Tusingham, passed us at that moment on her way to another table in the little dining room and smiled, having heard his rude remark. So I simply wrinkled my nose, finished my steak-and-kidney pie, and looked around for the tapioca pudding, which came all big and lumpy, the way I like it.

Although I heard nothing, I saw him out of the corner of my eye. He was laughing at me again. He looked much younger when he laughed like this.

During the two days I had known him, I found several moments such as this one, when his abrupt manner and "foreign look" seemed to thaw and he was quite civil and oddly attractive. And then too, I could never forget how safe I had felt in awakening to his protection after the shooting. Even in this deadly silence he was comforting when the only sound I could hear was a dreadful roaring, like wind in a cave.

I told him now as he watched me eat the pudding, "My head must be hollow."

"May one ask why?"

I grinned ruefully. "Because I keep hearing sounds like wind in a hollow cave."

I thought he would laugh again, but he didn't. Everything about him seemed to stop, even his breathing. He looked at me, and I kept waiting for his lips to move.

"Well, does that mean I may hear soon?" I ventured finally, wondering if I had only thought the words previously and not spoken them aloud.

"It means you may be in great—" Dr. Brandt broke off and shrugged, deliberately changing his mood. "No matter. It was inevitable."

"Shall I call the inspector and tell him?" I asked.

He looked at me straight, rather unnervingly. "You must make me a promise. A solemn promise. You understand?"

I agreed with some foreboding.

"Excellent. Promise that if the hearing returns you will not tell anyone but me."

"Of course. No one else need know anyway." I glanced at Miss Tusingham, whose bright little eyes were busy over the menu. "Except your nurse."

"I said *no one*. It is not a thing that should be known. There would be talk. You understand me?"

"I think so." I didn't, though. I couldn't quite picture me, Nona O'Carty, the object of daggers and guns when I hadn't been witness to any more than a coat sleeve, an arm-length, and a few sentences of dialogue.

The next time Detective Inspector MacLeish came to the hotel, which was the day after, I ran to meet him in the dark-paneled little hall.

"Please, couldn't I go on with my tour soon? Say, next Monday? I'm dying to see Europe, and the time is so short before I have to go home."

"My dear Miss O'Carty!" Inspector MacLeish protested, pronouncing my name so emphatically that I could not mistake his words. He looked friendly but official.

I sighed and thought, *You want to ask me questions
again. Those same tiresome questions. Not even a new
one.*

But unfortunately, I realized I had spoken the words
aloud, for Inspector MacLeish's blue eyes crinkled
pleasantly in his ruddy, well-scrubbed face and he
said, "One or two new questions, perhaps. Otherwise,
I'm afraid, the same tiresome matters."

"Yes, but can I go on with my trip? The Riviera, the
Rhine, Paris, places like that. Because if I'm not back
at my desk in the studio on May fifteenth, I'll lose my
job, and I just can't afford to do that. It's a very good
job."

Someone behind me put a hand on my shoulder, a
heavy hand whose pressure I recognized, a hand that
had begun to affect me noticeably. I turned to see what
Dr. Brandt had to say to me.

"Why not help the Inspector with these little questions? Something may come of the conversations one
day. Perhaps today. We do not know quite which statement is of importance. And then, the good inspector
will let you go your way. Isn't it so, Inspector?"

Just a thread of a frown crossed the Inspector's forehead, and I realized with a little jolt of surprise and
uneasiness that he did not really like Dr. Brandt, even
though they apparently worked together. Or maybe he
just didn't like the doctor's protective attitude toward
me.

I said, "I'll be happy to help you in any way. Only
I think I've told you everything I know. And I really
do intend to go on with my trip. No matter what."

Inspector MacLeish nodded. "Perfectly true, Miss
O'Carty. Still, there may be some clue somewhere that
has escaped us until this moment." He brightened then.
"But there is nothing in the book of rules that says we
may not see you safely to some little place on the Con-
tinent. Matter of fact, there is a little pension on the
Italian Riviera that would just suit . . . Sometime soon."
As I got excited and started to thank him, he put up his

hand, reminding me, "But I'll only do so if you help me about those details of the Putney business."

"Such a flattering deal!" I murmured. Then, as I felt Dr. Brandt's fingers tighten their hold on my shoulder, I glanced at him, wincing at the tight pressure. "Is it all right, Doctor? I feel fine. Honestly, I do. I'm perfectly fit to travel if I just allow for not hearing people."

Under the level, too-innocent gaze of Inspector Mac-Leish, Dr. Brandt reddened slightly and removed his fingers from my shoulder. "Certainly," he said. "It is as the inspector says. If the place is kept secret, and if a physician is there to—to take care of you . . . The inspector no doubt plans to make it appear that you have not left England. This trick has been played before, I believe."

"And successfully," said Inspector MacLeish, a little more decisively than he need have done. From which I suspected that he did not wish me to know of the "trick" Dr. Brandt had betrayed to me. I would be smuggled out of the country, no doubt, and some woman would remain here in my place. I did not care how it was done, so long as I got a chance to see a little more of the world before I returned home for that long, long wait until the next time I had enough money for such a trip.

"Aha, Miss!" Nurse Tusingham called to me later as we passed in the hall. "How the face glows! There must be a man."

"No. I'm going on with my tour. And soon," I told her gaily.

"Lucky you. Wish I could get away. There's a place in Torquay I'd give a bit to stop at again. Can't, though. I've the patients to attend, worse luck." A lot of this I could only guess at, for she talked rapidly and was difficult to follow. But I got the general drift.

Late the next day as I passed the open door to the hotel lounge, I saw both Dr. Brandt and Nurse Tusingham with their heads together discussing some cases, no doubt, and in a very animated way, for the air was full of hand motions, very foreign.

Inspector MacLeish, who had been making mysterious arrangements for my protection, saw the direction of my glance and said something, then remembered and tapped my arm.

"Interesting sort of chap, Max Brandt. They don't often get anyone with his qualifications down in Richmond."

"He's been very good to me," I said firmly. "He should have a fine office in Harley Street, or wherever. He's quite wonderful."

"A bit of a Gothic grumbler, I'm afraid," said my companion. And then, as I started to answer, calling him by his title, the inspector surprised me by saying in a rather winning way, "I'm not a bobby placing you in custody, Miss O'Carty. Could you call me 'Scotty,' do you think?"

I had no objection, although the name Scotty MacLeish struck me as awfully silly, and he had the grace to laugh about it with me. But soon I was busy thinking about the casual way he kept going back to the crime in the Putney stationer's shop.

"It's a silly business. I hate to dwell on it," he said.

"I know," I said with a great sigh. "I've thought and thought, but I can't dredge up any more clues. Doctor Brandt thinks I'm in danger from that man. I'm not afraid, though, if you say I'm under guard."

He looked mischievous. "Have you seen Alfred Skipton, the hall porter?"

"That funny little man who polishes the shoes in the hall at night?"

"None other. Looks harmless, doesn't he?"

"You don't mean he's the one! But shouldn't a guard be big and tough?"

Scotty MacLeish smiled. "Skipton is tough, right enough. His mother was born in County Mayo. That should satisfy a good Irish girl like you."

"Well, I should hope so! County Mayo, is it? Wait till Father hears that."

He put his hand out, touching mine lightly. "Please. You must not tell your father or anyone else, including those at the hotel. You understand this is for your safety."

His expression, the seriousness of his usually kind and gay face, shook me. I still couldn't quite understand or appreciate the deadliness of the atmosphere around me.

"Doctor Brandt said the same thing. He wanted me to keep quiet about everything. Sometimes," I ventured, hoping to get a little inside information, "I wonder if the doctor doesn't know more than he tells me."

"How do you mean?"

"Oh, you know," I went on vaguely. "He has something to do with your government."

Scotty took a long time before confessing. "He's done a good bit for us. A brilliant man. German background, but during the war he conducted an exceedingly active underground movement in Berlin and in East Prussia. An anti-Nazi almost from his boyhood."

I didn't think that being an anti-Nazi automatically qualified him as an extremely democratic person today. I was thinking of all the propaganda I had read about anti-Nazis who had been Communists, and still this hadn't interfered with their underground activities. However, no doubt the British Government knew what it was doing.

"But what in the world is he doing here in Richmond, Surrey? I'd think he could be of better use somewhere in—"

"Men in his profession outlive their uses," he remarked briefly.

"Doctors outlive their usefulness?"

"His other uses. He has been enormously helpful to us. One day, of course, they'll get him. In the meanwhile, his cover is in Richmond."

That silenced me. This Scotty MacLeish looked so

nice, so pleasant and easygoing, that I was disappointed to find him just as cynical as the rest of these secret agents and what-nots in real life. I was used to movie CID men who were sympathetic.

Presently, he asked me for what must have been the hundredth time to "Tell me in your own words precisely what the man in the tweed coat said."

I told him. I don't think I added anything I hadn't said before.

Suddenly the door of the lounge was pushed wide-open with a quick, impatient gesture that must have made a disturbance, because Scotty MacLeish looked around with the only jerky, unprepared gesture I had seen him make.

Dr. Max Brandt came striding toward us without even glancing at the inspector. "Come along, Nona. Too many questions. You belong in bed." This time he gave Scotty the most contemptuous look, making me think of an East European stereotype: severe, with a hint of menace that was only slightly belied by the look of concern in his eyes.

I felt I owed it to Scotty to say, "It was really my fault. We were just talking about—" I remembered we had been discussing Max Brandt himself and stopped self-consciously.

Making it difficult for the inspector to see and speak to me, Dr. Brandt drew me away insistently, saying something to Scotty over my head. The Inspector answered him and then made no effort to stop us. Whatever he said to me I couldn't tell, because I was being hurried along. The back of the hall was too dim for me to read Dr. Brandt's lips, so we made no conversation.

In my room Dr. Brandt, who was studying me with a disconcerting stare, put the back of his hand against my forehead with surprising tenderness and said in what I'm sure must have been a stern voice, "You are feverish. How do you feel?"

I raised my own hand, tested his rather unofficial

diagnosis, and found that he was right. I suppose I had been too excited over the possibility of seeing the Riviera, but there was, behind every move, every shadow, a prickling fear. Mr. Putney's murderer, who had every reason to kill me, his witness, was still free somewhere, perhaps very near. That alone was enough to give me a fever.

"The inspector will leave the guard for me all the time, night and day, won't he?" I asked Dr. Brandt as he turned on the lights in my room. The warm glow of the lamp gleamed momentarily on the broad, oddly Slavic planes of his face, and then, as he moved across the room to the window, these very features caught the shadows again. The harsh lips, the deep set of his eyes, the high-boned cheeks were all exaggerated to a sinister degree, and I stared at him, frowning.

It was this, I suppose, that made me suddenly cautious when Dr. Brandt remarked casually, "Without doubt. He did not say. I imagine it is not always the same one, though. These people have certain—I believe you call them 'shifts.' Inspector MacLeish will have told you whom to trust, naturally, among the personnel?"

"Oh yes. He is—" Almost too late I recalled Scotty MacLeish's stern instruction to me on this matter. Already I had given away the sex of Alfred Skipton, the "hall porter" who had been assigned to guard me, and I lamely tried to recover from this slip. "He—the inspector—is very nice, I think." I flattered myself that I had got out of that rather sneakily.

The doctor looked out the windows in both directions, then pulled them shut, locked them, and pulled the gaudy cretonne curtains closed. He asked me if I would take some mild sedative capsules, but being always mindful of things I read and heard about anything of the sort, and aware that Mother would never approve, I refused him politely.

"Now. You will go to bed," he told me, with just the suggestion of gentleness in his eyes to soften his hard manner. "And a tray of light supper will be brought to you. Should you prefer that it be brought by anyone special in the household? Because of your hearing, it must be someone with a key."

I wondered if this was a not-too-clever way to find out whom Scotty MacLeish had assigned to guard me, so although I was much too tired to be coy, I said as sweetly as I could, "I imagine you would be much too busy with your patients to bring it yourself, Doctor Brandt. Maybe your nurse might do it."

He paused, and for a moment we looked at each other. I had a very odd sensation. I remember wondering if he had forgotten what we were talking about, or even if he himself was having trouble with his hearing. He looked perfectly expressionless. Then he smiled. "My nurse is even busier than I. But once I have brought your tray, no one else enters. Have I your promise?"

It was an easy promise. I made it and he was gone. I thought a hot bath would do me more good than anything, but the bathtub was down the hall, and I didn't intend to wander about half-dressed in badly lighted halls. I undressed, got into bed, and fell asleep almost at once with the lamp on. I made it a habit now, during this spell of my deafness, always to have a light on somewhere. The most horrifying experience I had faced in the past few days had not been the actual attack on me, but the sensation of finding myself both deaf and in the dark. It was the closest thing to being dead that I could imagine.

Someone in my dreams knocked on the door several times, but I was too muddled to realize that I could not actually hear if anyone did knock. The room became increasingly stuffy, and I was used to sleeping with the window open.

I was still half-asleep, when several shadows crossed between me and the light. This silent but disturbing intrusion on the warm light of my room aroused me on the instant, and I sat straight up in bed. The sight I saw reassured me. In spite of Dr. Brandt's belief that she would be too busy, Nurse Tusingham came bustling in, followed by my protector, Alfred Skipton. I could almost hear the comforting rustle of the nurse's stiff uniform, completed by the nunlike headdress that could not keep her yellow hair from glistening in the lamplight.

The little Irishman had his hands full of shoes, apparently collected along the hall, although I did wonder if this was merely window dressing, since my bedside clock read eight-fifteen, a little early for making such collections. He glanced at me only briefly, but his big smile, which uncovered various toothless spaces in the front of his cavernous mouth, was so contagious that it raised my spirits immensely. I felt sure that he was Irish and that since the nurse's presence prevented him from revealing himself as more than a mere escort for her, he was giving me a bit of the true Irish charm.

Nurse Tusingham showed me the tray before laying it on the writing desk. There were slices of cold York-shire beef, succulent ham, a covered bowl steaming hot, which was probably soup, and an enormous pot of tea under a tea cozy. Miss Tusingham indicated that this would remedy all ills, and then, speaking very distinctly and I'm sure very loudly, she said, "I'm going to take your temperature, child, and then you are to eat what you can, and sleep." As she got out her thermometer she patted the tea cozy with her free hand. "And pots of tea. Just what you need for a good rest, child. Ah!" She examined the thermometer, and I took this chance to look at the hall porter. He nodded ever so slightly, still grinning, and put up two fingers in the Churchill victory sign behind her head.

An instant later Nurse Tusingham looked up and rustled her ample form around the room, puffing up the cushion on the one comfortable chair and straightening the cretonne curtains, glancing out the window and shivering.

"A bit of a chill out," she remarked, clutching her

shoulders to demonstrate. Then, after patting the bed covers where my legs made a lump under the sheets, she pointed to the door and mouthed distinctly, "Lock it!" Pushing the porter out ahead of her, she followed him.

I got out of bed, went over and turned the key in the lock, then took the key out and put it under my pillow. I did not feel up to chewing and eating the meat, but the soup was a splendid, thick sort of mulligan with potatoes and cabbage and bits of ham in it, and I ate a whole bowl full. I drank a little tea because it was hot and drove away the shivers, but it was strong the way the English like it, and I left most of it.

Warm and pleasantly aglow with soup and contentment at the thought of that comfortable bed, I got in and pulled the covers up. There was a light across the street in front of the Tudor inns, and it seeped in around the curtains at my window. Encouraged by this, I made myself turn out the lamp near the bed, and after a few minutes of forcing myself to get used to the semi-dark, I closed my eyes and went to sleep.

Sometime later, I was surprised at how chilly it became in my dream. I crawled down under the covers. But something disturbed my sleep, for I awoke to a sight that stunned me so much that my vocal cords refused to work and I felt myself gasping, wordlessly mouthing sounds in the most deadly panic I had known in my life.

Chapter Four

SOMETHING lean and dark and only vaguely silhouetted by the strips of light from the street lamp was huddled on my windowsill, with the cretonne curtains half-shrouding the creature. It put me in mind of a gigantic black jungle cat hunched and ready to spring. Even the claws, or one claw, sparkled in the light. It was a knife of some kind, long and surprisingly slender.

I remember that as I watched, stupefied for an instant, my body was terribly cold and stiff. Even if I tried, I could not move fast enough to avoid that knife. My only hope was that, since my bed was in the darkest half of the room, this creature did not yet know I was watching him. Having come in from the light of the street lamp, the creature had trouble getting his bearings. There were only seconds left to me. I shook off my paralysis and scrambled out of bed on the side nearest the door, shrieking like a banshee.

Waving the lethal needle-sharp knife, the creature leaped halfway across the room at me with a feline speed and grace, and then everything happened so fast that I saw it all from the floor, where the impetus of the intruder's leap had knocked me. Two men, Dr. Brandt and my little Irish hall porter, rushed into the room. While the doctor leaped upon my assailant, the porter just rolled me out of the way, and I lay there shaking.

The fight between Dr. Brandt and the strange creature with the knife was horrible. I cried out to the porter to help Dr. Brandt, but he remained where he

was, a shield between me and the two writhing there
with their own lives and mine at stake.

I saw the knife blaze in the streak of light from the
hall as it flashed between the two figures. I screamed
again, the more desperately because I heard no sound
pour from my throat.

Shadowy figures gathered, shifted, and circled in the
hall, but in spite of my frantic pleas, no one did anything to come between Dr. Brandt and the assassin. The
glistening knife vanished between their bodies, and in
the roaring silence I made out the black creature who
seemed to leap in the air and then collapse in an awk-
ward heap, so close to me that I felt the stinging slap
of his hand thrown hard across my arm, his flesh still
cold and damp from the foggy spring night.

Someone snapped on the overhead light, and I saw
Nurse Tusingham in the doorway, excitedly questioning Dr. Brandt. The doctor, breathless and disheveled,
ignored her and turned the invader over. We all saw
that the knife had broken off, the blade partially buried
in the unknown man's body below the breastbone,
horribly, sickeningly. . . .

But even so, it might have been worse. It might
have been Dr. Brandt whom I saw lying there like
that. Or me. Or me!

The room was soon full of people, and I can't remember very much that happened afterward in the
confusion, except that Inspector MacLeish came, and
there was a good deal of quiet, confidential talk between
him and Dr. Brandt, who must have explained a dozen
times just how the intruder had happened to fall upon
his own knife. It was, they told me, one of the few
wounds that would be likely to bring instant death.

From the various scrambles of conversation I was
able to understand, I felt that they had expected some
such visit by the murderer, that men had been posted
outside any of the possible entrances, and that the windows of my room had been securely locked. I knew
that Dr. Brandt had locked them and could testify to

as much. But somehow, when the cat creature came, he must have found them unlocked. There were no signs of broken latches or sills.

When I had got over my terror and could really do a little thinking, I wondered that they were all so much more concerned over other matters, such as the killing of my would-be murderer. As for me, I was delighted, in spite of the nasty way he had died. And it made me doubly proud of Dr. Max Brandt. I thought him quite the bravest man I'd ever known. But here they were in the middle of the night, and in my room, still fussing because the awful creature was dead.

"Pure rotten luck," murmured Scotty to Dr. Brandt. "Now we've no way of knowing the straight of it or who's back of him."

"Bad business all around, I must say," Nurse Tusingham put in as she bustled about tucking me secretly into bed again after I had tossed and turned a little too much to suit her.

Scotty and Dr. Brandt both glanced at her, the inspector frowning. Dr. Brandt, looking tired and worn, as well he might, merely gave her an indifferent look before he drank from a steaming cup of tea. Into the tea he poured either vodka or gin—I couldn't tell which, but he drank a great deal of it. The two men talked together frequently when the nurse left the room, from which I assumed that the doctor was actually in the confidence of Scotland Yard or whoever was handling the case of the dead Mr. Putney and the still-alive me. After a while, I went to sleep. Oddly enough, I didn't have any nightmares.

In the morning I was ordered by Dr. Brandt to stay in bed, where I was sitting up eating oatmeal when Scotty visited me again. When the doctor had gone to get some rest, Scotty told me to expect an examination by another physician in an hour or so.

I felt this was a reflection on my rescuer. "Why? Don't you trust Doctor Brandt?"

"Oh, quite. But you see, we're considering taking

you closer in custody, for your own protection. And we want to be sure that—"

"But you can't!" I cried. "My money is going to run out before I ever see Europe. Couldn't I go over to the Continent somewhere the way you said, and enjoy myself while I'm—I guess 'hiding out' is the proper term?"

He smiled. "Do you know what you are hiding out from?"

"The man in the pepper-and-salt coat, I guess."

"Much more than that, I'm afraid. You see, the man who died in this room last night was known to us. He is one of *them*."

"Them?"

"The other side."

I pretended to understand, but it was all very cloak-and-daggerish, and I half-thought he might be making an Englishman's idea of a joke. More than ever I wanted to get out of this country, where *they* went around killing people and trying to stab me. On the other hand, I couldn't bear the thought of returning to California without seeing at least a little bit of Europe.

"Is he a spy?" I asked straight out.

"*Was* would be the term. Not so much a spy as a useful tool of theirs. We've been hoping he'd lead us to more important fish."

I considered the matter. "This cat burglar man may have tried to kill me here, but he wasn't the man who killed Mr. Putney."

Inspector MacLeish looked at me in a penetrating way that made me realize that he could be dangerous. It was an odd sensation, but I did not hold this against him. Papa always insisted the English were tough. "How can you be sure he did not kill Putney? You didn't see the killer, or did you?"

I raised my chin and looked right back at him. "Because Mr. Putney's killer was bigger and probably much taller. After all, I know where his arm was when he had hold of the doorknob. The man last night wasn't nearly tall enough."

He nodded. "Perfectly sound reasoning. Anyway, the voice you described was not Eichler's voice. Your dead assassin, by the by, used that among other names."

"He looked to me like a cat burglar. In that tight black outfit. What a silly way to dress!"

He laughed at my comment but explained something technical that I didn't understand, about black leather making him slippery to hold and hard to see in the dark and I don't know what all. I was much more anxious to persuade them to let me go on to France and Italy, at least. It was ridiculous to be cooped up here exactly where these mysterious enemies knew I was, and I told Scotty so. To my surprise he agreed.

"No doubt of it. We must do something. Max believes there was no structural damage to your eardrums or, in fact, to your hearing. Is the scalp laceration healing satisfactorily?"

"Yes," I said eagerly, anxious to persuade him that I was well enough to travel. "It doesn't hurt at all. Either Doctor Brandt or Nurse Tusingham changes the bandages every day. It seems to be fine. I really should be hearing again any time."

"The more reason to keep you near at hand. For identification."

I made a face at this typically official reason for wanting me well again. "But don't you see? Unless you put me in prison or something, they will be able to get to me no matter what you do, so long as I am around here. Couldn't you put me somewhere within an hour's flying time from here or something? . . ."

"The west of England, perhaps. You'd like it there."

"No. No, you said the Riviera. In France. Or Italy. Some romantic place. And you could maybe spare Doctor Brandt to take me there and get me settled, just for a little while. I'll probably be able to hear—who knows?—in a week or less."

His faraway expression indicated that he was con-

sidering my idea, although he had caught the snub
about unromantic England. "You might find Cornwall
romantic. Most Americans do."

"But they'd be sure to look for me in England. Don't
you see? You said you'd take me to that pension on the
Italian Riviera. You promised!"

I knew I was being childish, but one upsetting thing
after another seemed to plot against me, and here I
had been thinking of that Riviera pension during every
waking minute. Now, to have it all dismissed, and all
this talk of Cornwall instead, was just too much! I had
my heart set on sunny Riviera beaches, quaint little
pensions, and sidewalk cafés. If I had wanted to go to a
place like Cornwall, I would have planned it that way."

"Well, well, we'll see," the inspector promised in
that pacifying way which is so annoying to hear.

"If you don't get me out of this foggy, depressing
place," I promised him seriously, "I'll leave by myself.
I mean it. How can I ever feel safe here again? If it
hadn't been for Doctor Brandt, I'd be dead now."

Scotty MacLeish flushed darkly and started to say
something, then broke off. "Very true. I'll see what
can be done. In any case, no one will enter your room
without one of our men being present."

"And the window?" I asked ironically.

"You will be moved to a room on the floor above as
soon as the doctors have completed their examination.
Impossible to reach the windows on that floor, even
for a cat burglar."

I knew I had cut him deeply by the reminder that
Dr. Brandt and not Scotty or his men had saved my
life, but if that was the only way to get out of here, I
was glad I had been so rude.

"I'll go up to that other room, but only temporarily.
You will arrange something . . . won't you?"

He said coldly, "If it is approved, you have my
word. Good day."

As I watched him go, I caught a glimpse of Alfred
Skipton hanging around in the hall. Poor man. What a

dull job! All during that morning, while Mr. Meighan and Dr. Angerstein examined me from head to toe and tested my ears, eyes, reflexes, and every inch of my skull, I kept remembering little Alfred Skipton trying to look busy while he guarded my door.

In the end the doctors merely confirmed the diagnoses of Dr. Brandt and the first ear specialists.

"Then why can't I hear?" I asked with what I considered great reasonableness.

Their answers—which had to do with my reflexes, the state of my nerves, the glancing blow of the shot, and numerous more-technical matters—were so complicated that I continued to rely upon Dr. Brandt's simple promise that I would hear quite suddenly, at any time. He did suggest, later in the day when he took me walking down Richmond Hill with Alfred Skipton tagging after us, that he be allowed to give out the information that I might never hear again.

"That isn't the truth, is it?" I asked suspiciously, staring hard at him to catch any betraying sign. But he shook his head. "It is for your safety, you understand? Why not let everyone—Skipton there, nurse Tusingham, all the employees—believe you may never hear again. I have discussed this with the physicians as well. It may turn away any more of those attacks on you."

"Do you honestly think Inspector MacLeish is right? That a gang of Communists is after me? What on earth could they have to do with the pepper-and-salt man killing Mr. Putney?"

He stopped and picked from a hedge a pretty yellow cup-shaped wildflower that reminded me of California poppies except that it was larger. As he stopped, I stopped, and Skipton, striding along behind us, had to put on the brakes fast to keep from running into us. I thought Dr. Brandt had forgotten my question as he casually handed me the flower, which I immediately treasured and determined to press and put in my diary.

But when we walked on and stood a few minutes looking down the embankment toward the lush green valley of the Thames, he said abruptly, "Neither Communists nor Tories nor Laborites come in gangs any more, my dear Nona."

"Covens?" I asked with great innocence, hoping to tease a smile out of him. "Oh, pardon me! That's quails that come in covens."

"You are probably thinking of coveys. Witches are found in covens, I believe."

"Seriously," I said, looking into his face with a gaze he couldn't evade. "Did you think what I overheard that day had to do with Communists?"

This time he did smile a little, but only, I think, at my manner, for he took my question quite seriously. "It is very probable. The man I killed was Horst Weichsmann, whom they used to call the Cat Man in Berlin. He has been of use to the Party for years."

"Of use!" I shuddered and then glanced at him curiously. "You knew him . . . in the old days?" I almost wished I hadn't asked; for it sounded like a trick question, as if I were trying to trap him into something.

I was relieved when he replied unhesitatingly with a grim smile, "I knew them all. Why do you ask?"

"Because Scotty—I mean, Inspector MacLeish—called him Eichler."

"He had a dozen aliases. The French knew him as the Fishing Cat. That is how he got into your room when the windows were locked, probably. The cat-burglar method of his. There are dozens like him."

"Don't say that!"

He pinched my chin and made me stare at him as he said very slowly for my perfect understanding, "That is why I wish it known that the new diagnosis is negative. You may never hear again. You understand the importance of this?"

"I . . . th-think so," I stammered, chilled to the bone by his manner as well as the grim threat that he had not uttered.

He studied my face for what seemed a long time to me, and I was very much aware of little Alfred Skipton at a slight distance from us, rocking impatiently on his heels. Dr. Brandt's fingers pinched my chin until it felt numb, but I did not mind. He was acting so odd that I didn't know what to expect when he lowered his head and, with surprising gentleness, kissed me on my cool, unprepared lips.

I didn't know what motive in this complicated man had prompted that slight touch which seemed to have no passion in it but only a sad, sweet tenderness left over from some gentler time in his life. So I tried to let him see my heart in my eyes as I said with grave politeness, "Thank you."

"Not at all," he returned with equal gravity. A moment later, he added, "Will you promise me something, Nona?"

"Of course."

"First, you are not going to that place with the CID people."

"But they said—"

"Believe me, they are only pacifying you. I want you to promise me you will not try to force the business of that trip."

I felt sick with disappointment. I had been so sure the promise had something to do with that kiss, perhaps even that he loved me a little bit. And all the time, he was only doing Scotty MacLeish's errands. Naturally, they didn't want me making scenes over that trip.

"But I want to go there. Or somewhere. I've lost so much of my vacation time that I'll never make it up. Why shouldn't I go there? I'll be perfectly safe. The inspector would see to that, wouldn't he?"

He looked down over the green vista to the river in the distance. When he turned back to me, he seemed to have made some vital decision. His harsh face was set. He put out his hand and cupped his palm over the back of my head. Then, his hand slipped down over the nape of my neck. A single gesture, and he could draw my head close in a gesture of love. Or, if

he were one of my enemies, he could easily strangle
me.

I thought it would amuse him if I made a joke of
his peculiar, unthinking gesture. "Do you intend to kiss
me or choke me, Doctor?"

He did not seem to understand me at first. Nor did
his expression reveal that he thought my remark at all
funny. Then, very slowly, he let me go. He looked over
my head, behind me. Skipton, my protector, had moved
forward.

I turned around quickly and waved him back. "It's
quite all right, you know. Max and I are good friends."

Dr. Brandt took my arm and hurried me along. I
watched to see what he would say. When there was no
question of Skipton's overhearing, I suggested hopefully, "Couldn't you go with me to that place the inspector knows about?"

"You don't understand. They know where you may
be taken. They will be waiting for you. Someone has
talked."

"How do you know?"

"Because the entire hotel is buzzing about it. And if
all those idiots know, you may be sure *they* know. It
was like that many years ago, when I worked with
them and . . . someone else died."

"In the underground?"

"In the war, yes."

We did not speak, or at least I did not see him
speak, as we walked into the busy street of the town.
When we passed Mr. Putney's stationer's shop, which
was still locked, with the shades drawn, I shuddered,
and he drew me closer to him.

"Where did you find me?" I asked, and he pointed
out the spot, half in and half out of the shop door, as
he explained. "I was returning from a case. My patient
had died in the night. I was in no pleasant frame of
mind. Then I saw you lying there."

"I'm glad it was you who found me," I murmured,
wishing that there was nothing else to trouble me and

that I could keep forever this unbelievable happiness of feeling his body beside me, his dear face, his comforting voice. What was that voice like? I wondered. A harsh, Germanic voice, probably. Or even Slavic. What was his past? Where was he born? What was his boyhood like?

"Someday I'll know all about you," I thought aloud. "I would love to know all about when you were a boy, what your world was like, why you went to work for British Intelligence, everything. All the little things that made you human. Even the bad things about you."

"God forbid!" he said, but softened this with a laugh. Then, quite suddenly, he seemed to have an idea and asked me a question almost as quickly and spontaneously as though he were suggesting that we take in the local movie. "Would you trust me to take you to the Continent?"

I was confused. "You mean the inspector would let you?"

"I mean would you trust *me?* The inspector has nothing to do with it."

It was an astonishing idea, enchanting, yet impossible. I made the obvious objection. "I couldn't travel with you."

"Why? Tell me why." I felt now that he was teasing me with that odd, straight, unsmiling face.

"For one thing, I hate to sound so mid-Victorian, but my parents definitely would not approve of it."

This time he did smile. "Of it, or of me? If the disapproval is not directed specifically at me, we may get around that, by—"

"No. No. I couldn't fool them."

"—by that mid-Victorian custom called marriage."

I did not understand this, and when he repeated it and I understood at last, I felt too shaken with excitement to do more than think up obstacles.

"You've known me such a short time. You know so little about me. How can you love me?"

"My dear Nona, who is talking of love? What has that to do with my offer?"

This was a dreadful letdown.

"But how could you marry me if you don't love me? I'm not rich. I mean, what other reason would you have?"

"To save your life and get you out of their reach, you little fool! Come along now. It's getting cold. I don't want you dying off of pneumonia before I can make my supreme sacrifice."

I didn't know what to say. I wanted terribly to marry him, but I wanted him to love me, and I wanted to have a long, romantic engagement, at the end of which would come a lovely church wedding, with the priest and all.

"Think it over," he told me, and added the sharp warning, "but if you utter one word of this conversation to anyone—including, in particular, friend MacLeish, I shall deny it all, and what is more, I shall prescribe some of the most foul-tasting drugs you have ever encountered. Added to which, there will be no tour of the Continent."

I was fairly sure he was teasing me, but something about the fixed expression of his eyes frightened me just a little, and I knew I would not dare betray his offer, even to Scotty.

Chapter Five

I NEVER knew whether Inspector MacLeish really intended to have me taken to the Riviera or whether it had been a lie from the first, a sop to me all along, but the official silence about my trip was my proof that Dr. Brandt had been right. Along with my disappointment in Scotty, my suspicions of the people at the hotel began to rise. If Max was right about the one matter, he was very probably right about the other. It was getting so that I could not trust anyone, except Max and myself.

All the evening after the doctor's strange but terribly tempting proposal to me, I kept watching everyone in the hotel, and it seemed to me that the more I considered them, the more suspiciously they behaved. I hoped to tell Dr. Brandt that he was right and to encourage him to see and know me better so that he might make everything right in his proposal by actually growing to love me. I was sure I loved him. All other "loves" in my life, such as they had been, paled beside the violence of the infatuation I felt for Max.

But suddenly, after that romantic offer to me, he became perverse, as if to tantalize me. He was with me only when necessary, in the morning and just before bedtime the next day, and always, true to his promise, with the most detestable medicines. I suspected this was a gesture to keep reminding me of his proposal.

Nurse Tusingham, at least, recognized my enormous preoccupation with the doctor. I met her late the next afternoon in the American Bar, where she said she was recuperating from her current patient over several "gin and its."

"That odd old pussy who has me in tow—'Meow, meow,' all day, all night! She was on a walking tour, mind. At seventy-eight. Broke her ankle, but you'd think it was her neck. Pity it wasn't. Have one, dearie?"

I looked around. Skipton wasn't in sight, but a big, pudgy, florid-faced man in the doorway smiled at me, and I realized he must be my Irishman's replacement on the other shift. For the past few days, whenever Skipton was out of sight, I had entertained myself by trying to guess which of the odd characters around the hotel was substituting for the Irishman. Once, it turned out to be a woman, a middle-aged and garrulous chambermaid who amazed me because her mouth was always going and yet, so far as I could tell, she said nothing that meant anything.

Nurse Tusingham eyed me with roguish good humor. "Looking out for Max, are you? He's off in one of his sulky moods, most like." She drank off what was left of her version of the martini and set the glass down hard on the worn oak bar. Automatically, the bored barman refilled it.

I asked for a shandygaff, partly because its lethal qualities were not on a par with those gin and its and partly because Papa, who could drink any man under the table, did not approve of "the good Irish" or any other hard liquor being wasted on females. I wanted very much to ask the nurse if she had heard anything about my leaving Richmond, but I did not dare to. I had promised both Scotty and Dr. Brandt. Scotty, of course, was hardly on speaking terms with me, and now, with Max Brandt off somewhere, I could not learn anything. The suspense was terrible.

I said this aloud. "The suspense is terrible," and Nurse Tusingham turned and looked at me.

She remarked with an understanding pat on my arm, "I understand how it is, lass. It's the not knowing. Any minute, day or night, one of them thugs creeps in, and you've bought it. It's enough to put you off your head just thinking about it." She leaned closer. Her breath was rank with the gin and vermouth she had been pouring in. I knew her job must be a very difficult one. But who could tell? It might have driven me to drink, as well. . . .

"Nona, me girl, what you need is to get away out of this accursed place. Away out. Maybe to . . . somewhere they never heard of you, so you can make a bit out of your trip-like."

"I couldn't agree with you more," I began eagerly. "I said just that to Inspector MacLeish last—" I stopped. Mother always said, "You'll not be stopping the Irish from their tongues wagging." And sure, it was true. I'd come that near to betraying the secret that might involve my life or death!

"So you've thought of it. Good girl." She peered into her drink, said something I couldn't understand, and then, remembering, looked at me again as she spoke. "Did you convince old Scotty? He's got a pretty hard head. Once he kept a witness holed up in Glasgow. I mean—really! The poor devil near went off the rails. Said he'd rather be done in by the spivs."

"Spivs?"

"This was right after VE Day. They were a bit much. That was before you were born, dearie."

I laughed. "Not quite before I was born, but just about. Anyway, the inspector doesn't want me to go far. Maybe up to London for a change. Anyway, I couldn't persuade him." And adding still another nail to the coffin of her wrong guess, I said gloomily, "Now they think I may not hear again—ever."

"Yes. I know."

She did not explain how she knew. I wondered if she believed me. I had the oddest feeling that behind her rosy pink face and all that yellow hair, so angelically set off by the nun's coif, there was a woman who cared deeply about things, a woman who had, perhaps, seen a great deal of suffering, which drove her to down these gin and its, as though they were water.

"You're the better for it, girl. Believe old Bertha," she went on, surprisingly. "All you hear when you've good ears is stuff you're the better for not hearing."

With my remembrance of Mr. Putney's shop I could almost agree with her. "But things like music and the sounds of the world around you," I explained. "I miss them. It's worst at night, when it's dark. It's like being in your coffin, buried. No sight. No sound."

She swallowed a big gulp of gin, then reminded me with those bugged-out round eyes of hers fixed on me, "Dearie, if you do get the sounds back and all ship-shape, you come tell old Bertha all about it. Because you'll need a deal more help than them stupid police'll give you. Max says they're not even giving you twenty-four-hour guards. Only at night. Nobody could be that dumb, even the police. . . . Is it true?"

This time I was ready for her. I gave a disconsolate shrug and murmured, "I guess so. They figure I'm safe as long as I can't hear. And if I never hear again—well . . ." I trailed off lamely, admiring my own skill at playing this new part.

"Just like I thought. They're idiots, all of them. You come to me if anything goes on that you don't like the look of. You'd ought to be out of the Isles, is what you'd ought to be."

I glanced at her, startled, then pretended to be observing the worn, rounded edge of the bar.

She persisted, "I know a couple of places that'd suit you right down to the ground. Just remember." She squeezed my hand in a tight, sweaty grasp, then swung away from the bar. "Got to get on my way now. Back to old pussy. Meow!" She hustled off. She was a very big woman. She walked big. It was a little frightening to see her from the back.

I was halfway through supper in the quaint little dining room that night, when Inspector MacLeish came in looking for me. I didn't want to keep up the feud with him and tried to be especially nice, for I had a guilty conscience about my private feelings for Max

Brandt. I asked Scotty to join me for dessert, but he said tapioca pudding, our staple dessert, was not in his diet. He did accept tea, however, and sat down opposite me at my table. Ever since the Eichler-Weichsmann cat burglar had visited me, I always found a place with my back to a wall when I was in a public place. This also made it easier for Dr. Brandt or Scotty or Nurse Tusingham to talk with me in confidence, since the other tables were out of hearing.

"You win," Scotty said now as I was getting ready to bring up fresh reserves in my argument for that Riviera trip. If only I could manage this without putting Max Brandt to any trouble, he could hardly be marrying me to get me out of the country. Then, if he still wanted to marry me, without strings attached, I would marry him in a minute.

I was so surprised over Scotty's remark, however, that I barely kept from thanking him too loudly. At his raised hand I subsided and asked in a low voice, "Is it to be the pension on the Italian Riviera?"

"Well, not precisely that. But a place you'll like quite as well—in London. But very safe," he added quickly, seeing my movement, which actually signified my final, total loss of faith in Scotty MacLeish.

Numbed by the realization, I could do nothing but cling tenaciously to the knowledge that Max Brandt had predicted and expected this, that he either loved, or at least wanted, me and would be in every way the answer to all my dreams of noble Gothic heroes.

Scotty looked around. After a first curious glance at us, no one else in the dining room seemed interested. The trouble was, you never could tell. Any one of Scotty's mysterious *"them"* would certainly be as good an actor as I was. Max had reminded me of that. If they were in this room, I would probably be the last to recognize them. Scotty, however, appeared to tabulate every face and set it away in his mind.

"Yes, I think we may count on this place in London, at least for a short time. The personnel belong to us. It is for your own safety, you understand, Nona, a kind of hospital. But not the sort you fear," he added, as I exclaimed something inarticulate, I'm sure, with the shock of what I considered his betrayal.

If he was pleasant to me, he probably thought, I would be satisfied with my little taste of foreign intrigue and be happy to testify and get home to safe, dull, secure California. I did not disillusion him. But I pinned all my thoughts and hopes now on Max Brandt, remembering the way he looked at me when we passed briefly in hallways or in the dining room and the way he made a funny little expression of distaste when he forced me to drink those detestable-tasting liquids, supposed to be vitamins, which invariably reminded me of his promise.

Until Scotty MacLeish confessed that my romantic little Continental tour was to end in a "hospital but not the sort I feared," I had hesitated, feeling all the guilt of betraying him with my trust in Max Brandt, and guilty too because each of my daily letters to my parents and all my thoughts night and day were filled with Max Brandt.

Max was away attending several patients at the local hospital that evening, and I did not know how much he had heard or guessed of the conversation that killed all my last hopes of Scotty and his precious guardians of me. When Nurse Tusingham, accompanied by the ubiquitous little Alfred Skipton, visited me at bedtime, testing my reflexes and inquiring closely about any return of hearing, all I could think of was whether I should see Max that night, no matter how late.

I did not see him after all, though I lay awake so long that I naturally overslept in the morning, and there was Dr. Max Brandt standing at the side of my bed when I awoke. I looked around quickly, hardly daring to hope that he was actually seeing me alone. Whatever trick he had played on the garrulous chambermaid whose turn it was to watch me, she was not within hearing now.

"Temperature normal," he said in a professionally indifferent way, shaking the stupid glass thermometer. It was terribly annoying to me, because I hoped he would have something to say in answer to Scotty Mac-Leish's intentions. However, he did not look down at me and ask casually, "Do you have your passport, or did the police take it away?"

My pulse began to react violently, but thought I had better not pursue the matter until he gave me another clue. "In my purse, hanging on a hook under my coat over there."

He looked amused, and after an abortive effort or two, located the correct handbag, my old black plastic one with the thread along the handle beginning to rip.

"Good." He waved it briskly, and in a tone just as conversational, said, "Have you changed your mind?"

Confused, I asked, sitting up abruptly, "About what?"

He stepped over to the foot of my bed and looked down at me, and for just a second or two I thought there was a very special expression that softened his entire face and made him seem younger. But then he spoiled it by slapping my feet with my passport.

"Get up now, lazybones. Comb your pretty hair and powder your funny nose. I always insist on marrying only well-groomed women."

This was my opportunity. I got out of bed and ran to him barefooted, shiny-nosed.

"Please tell me. I can't marry you if you don't love me. When you are married by a priest, it is forever."

He smiled, then shook his head. "But we won't be married by a priest. Priests talk. First we will be married in a registry office."

"Oh, but—"

"Then, when you are safe, when there is no longer danger, a priest, if you like. If I am . . . available."

I hardly noticed that. "I can't marry you," I said sternly, swallowing hard to give myself the courage to

turn down the proposal of this man whom I felt I
would always love.

He looked surprised, as if we had spent a long and
intimate engagement and my statement now was un-
heard-of. "Why not?"

"Because I can't marry a man who doesn't love me."

He appeared undecided whether to give me up as a
hopeless case or to pause and make one more effort
to combat a senseless objection. "My dear Nona, my
feelings have nothing whatever to do with the matter.
I would not marry you if I did not wish to. There. Does
that satisfy you?"

I turned away so I need not hear any more. I really
wanted to cry, but it was such an absurd and childish
reaction in a time like this that I was able to sniff hard
and forget tears. How could I marry a man who married me as some sort of duty? He might even learn to
hate me in time. I had taken several steps before I felt
his hand upon my own, holding me back, trying hard
to be gentle, a task obviously difficult to one of his
forceful nature.

"Nona! Wait. Listen to me."

I felt as I studied his face that for the first time he
was revealing something of the self behind those harsh,
embittered features. Sometimes in the days we had
known each other, I had caught a hint of an old memory in the darkness of his deep-set eyes, but now for
this brief time, I felt that he had removed the careful
mask of years.

"Nona, when I saw you in the doorway of Putney's
shop that morning, I thought for a moment you were
. . . a very dear person I once knew. That is why I
saved you. There was no other reason. I knew even
then that it would further involve me, and endlessly,
with the police. I am not a hero. But I don't intend that
you shall be executed as she was."

"Executed!" The word was brutal, horrible. And
true, of course. They intended to execute me. But my

cry, and even more, my revulsion, had already driven Max Brandt back behind that harsh, sardonic mask.

"Did I say 'execute'? Just a figure of speech. Good people don't execute, do they? They merely punish the offender. Don't be frightened. No one is going to kill you if you . . ." He smiled. "If you make me a good wife and can cook in a fair way. I am very fond of potato pancakes and red cabbage." He paused and gave me a quick, sharp, observing look. "Unless, of course, it is me you are frightened of."

"No, no!" I threw my arms around him impulsively, hoping by my arms, my body, my enthusiasm, to warm him to that man I had briefly surprised behind the mask of half a harsh lifetime. "Oh, Max, if you will only let me love you! I'll make you happy again. And I'm a very good cook."

He was surprised by my gesture, but then he pulled me to him. We did not even kiss at first, but only drew some necessary strength from each other.

"Are you happy now, my suspicious little one?" he asked finally. "Are you quite sure that I want to keep you safe, not for your sake, but for my own?"

"I wouldn't have it any other way. When is it to be? When do we leave? How will we throw Skipton off our trail?"

He sighed and complained, "You ask too many questions. Go and dress. And remember—say nothing to anyone."

"I promise."

He kissed me again before I could get away from him, but I did not object to that. I thought I must surely be the happiest girl in the British Isles on this particular drizzly spring morning. At the door he waved my passport, smiled in the way that I had rapidly learned to treasure, and said, "I will see you as soon as things are arranged, Ilona."

My difficulty in reading his lips at that distance made me ask him apologetically, "What did you call me, darling?"

"Nona. What else would I call you? Be a good girl and remember—don't pack. Don't do anything that will suggest you are leaving. Our lives may depend on it." He had been very businesslike up to now, but here he studied me somberly while I shifted from one foot to the other, wondering. Had he been an artist I would have said he framed my face to paint it, or to remember it. Then he opened the door and left, abruptly.

Chapter Six

IT SEEMED to me long afterward, that the day I planned to run away from Richmond Hill was full of confusion from its beginning in the morning, when Max made the first move, until late in the night, when, instead of being in the air over the Channel and flying to Paris, I found myself in quite a different and, to me, far more sinister place, quite alone.

I could hardly eat breakfast after Max's business-like handling of the most important event in my life, my marriage. To make matters worse, when I was in this state of nerves Nurse Tusingham sat down at my table and began by complaining about the condition of the eggs and the quality of the sausages.

"And I'm not the only one, dearie. Look at that plate of yours. You've not eaten a mouthful. Look at those eggs. Something on your mind, I expect."

"I expect," I said absently, and then, recalling Max's order not to let anyone get suspicious, I added, "Besides, I really have been eating. I had porridge before the eggs. I'm just not used to such big breakfasts. At home, all I have is doughnuts and coffee."

"That has a frightfully Yankee sound," she murmured with strong disapproval, "and I shouldn't think you'd find it very nourishing."

I rather resented this gratuitous advice and felt that I had to defend my habits.

"I've always been extremely healthy, so it can't do too much damage." I pretended to eat some of the egg but was deeply aware of her round, bulbous little eyes watching my every move.

She said suddenly, "Why did you say that?"

"Say what?" It seemed to me now that since I had been having trouble with my hearing, I often said things aloud that I intended only to think.

"That you ate porridge this morning. You didn't, you know. I was sitting right over there and I saw."

"Does it really matter?" I asked boldly, nervous enough and angry enough to be belligerent.

She leaned forward across the table. I found her pretense of confidential gossip even worse than her general effusiveness. "It is a symptom, dearie. Did you know that? It means you're worried about something. You see, that's why you dropped your fork. You're as nervous as a bride."

The fact that she was right did not help me to calm my nerves, but I kept religiously in mind the warning by Max. I did not betray anything except my own condition.

"It is hardly surprising that I am a little nervous. It isn't every day that gangs of murderers pursue me and I am nearly killed—though almost every day," I added as an afterthought.

As I excused myself, got up, and left the little dining room, it seemed to me that everyone there was watching me, the way the creepy Miss Tusingham had watched me before I knew it this morning. I wandered out in front of the hotel, hoping I would soon receive word from Max and end this suspense. Where was he? I wondered if anyone suspected him of his plan as I was sure they suspected me.

The sun was trying to shine in a watery way, and I hoped it was a good omen, but when I looked behind me, there was Alfred Skipton lingering just inside the doorway; and what was worse, Nurse Tusingham, apparently free of her "old pussy with the broken ankle" came sauntering out past me, sniffing the air and strolling down the hill toward the village center.

In my ears there was a dreadful noise again, the roaring that sounded like air rushing through a cave. Then the noise went away and there came the now

familiar "dead sound." Silence. Even now, at this instant, my would-be assassin might be hanging about
somewhere here on this peaceful little hill, waiting to
get a perfect shot at me. Panic-stricken, I turned and
ran past Skipton, in through the dark-paneled hall, and
up the stairs to my room.

There was a note under my door. My fingers shook
so much that it was difficult to get the note unfolded.
It merely said, "2 P.M. A little walk." I sat down and
prepared to wait the tense, nervewracking hours until
we took our little walk and changed my life forever.

A chain had been put on my door since the night
attack, and although I could not hear the door when it
was pushed open an inch on the chair, I could always
sense when it was happening.

My lunch tray had been taken away shortly after
noon, practically untouched. I couldn't force myself to
eat anything. I kept thinking of how disappointed
Mother would be, and even Papa, that they could not
attend my wedding. Well, we must simply be married
properly, later, when we weren't running away.

He was early! My night-table clock said 12:15. I
saw the door open an inch or two, and I moved away
from the window, hurrying to let him in. I had on my
everyday black coat with the high collar, and my
pumps that were the best for walking, in spite of their
high heels. And then I went to the door and it was the
garrulous chambermaid. I was so disappointed that I
nearly closed the door on her, but she put her strong
hands out.

"Please, Miss, you are to be moved to safety in London. They're waiting down in Richmond. Can you
come at once?"

They seemed in a terrible hurry. I wondered why
the suddenness. My suspicions, never really asleep,
were now aroused again.

"I'm not quite ready. I mean, I've been looking for
my hat." I did not remove the chain from the door.

"You have your coat on!" she exclaimed, peering at

me with some difficulty. "Were you expecting to leave with us, Miss?"

I fluttered around the room pretending to look for my nonexistent hat, while I let her talk on. She had obviously forgotten that I couldn't hear or understand her unless I looked at her. So I did not look. After a few minutes, she rattled the door. It must have made a great racket, because I saw the chain pulling tight. I got into half the room she couldn't see, and wrote on the back of the note from Max, "12:20 to London. Police order." I didn't know what else to do.

Having killed all the time I could, I went out with the chambermaid and down the stairs. I asked where Alfred Skipton, her relief man, was, and she said, "Off-duty." I was sardonically happy to know that Skipton had regular hours, regularly enforced.

We passed the desk clerk and I said to him, "Tell Doctor Brandt I won't be using his prescription. I am going to London. Where am I going in London?" I asked the pseudo-chambermaid.

"Inspector MacLeish has it in charge. He will know," the woman replied.

I gave the note to the clerk, who promised that Dr. Brandt would get it.

The woman urged me on out. She seemed in a great hurry. At the curb was a large, black closed car of some kind whose make I didn't recognize, but it reminded me of the ancient taxicabs I had seen in London. The rear door was open, and a woman looked out, taking my hand as I approached. It was too late to turn back when I realized the hand that helped me into the back seat was that of Nurse Tusingham, complete in her saintly uniform with its nunlike, stiff headpiece that didn't conceal her fluffy hair.

My first thought, idiotic as it seems in retrospect, was that Nurse Tushingham was acting in Max's behalf and that this was all a part of his plan for our escape from surveillance. I got into the stuffy car, which seemed almost shrouded in black to me, and watched Nurse Tushingham wave to the chambermaid, whose air of command throughout had been most unlike her obscure role. Just as the car started to pull away, I saw Alfred Skipton returning to the place where he always stood at this hour of the day, lounging there as if waiting for me to come out for my usual walk.

I watched him for a few seconds, stupefied, not sure at all what was happening. He asked the chambermaid something. She pointed upward at the Tudor front of the old building, and he stepped out onto the sidewalk, peering up at what very probably was my room. He asked another question, she nodded, and he stepped back to his post against the street wall near the door.

The car in which I was jammed next to Nurse Tusingham took off suddenly with a terrible jarring and shaking. The nurse said something to me, which I didn't understand. I asked who our chauffeur was; I didn't recognize the man. And this time she had nothing to say.

Disastrously late, I realized that I had been hoodwinked from the very start of this expedition. If Skipton stood there looking up at my room, he must expect me to be there. It was barely possible that Max had sent his nurse for me, but I did not really believe it now. Very probably, this was a trick by my old enemy with the pepper-and-salt coat, and its object was my death.

Shaking inwardly, though my face was reasonably calm, I shoved my telltale hands into my coat pockets and sat back, pretending to be comfortable and confident of my destination.

"Ah, good, girl," said the nurse in her hideously soothing way. "You'll be safe and sound now."

I gave myself one last chance to believe in and to prove the innocence of this trip. With Skipton still on duty back at the hotel, I thought, this proved that the garrulous chambermaid was a liar, so her instructions that we were going into London at Police orders must be lies as well. The only safe alternative to the police was Max. I decided to test Max Brandt's part in this. I remarked ever so casually to Bertha Tusingham, "I wonder what Doctor Brandt's plans are." I assumed that if she was taking me at his directions, she would mention something of his idea about our destination. If not, then I had not given away the plan of flight between Max and me.

I held my breath as I watched the nurse's lips for her answer. A word or two about our meeting, that she did this at his orders, and I would feel safe. She said instead, " 'Fraid Doctor Brandt's a bit of a trouble-maker, dearie. There's a hint going the rounds—just a hint, mind!—that he's outlived his usefulness."

So this was not a part of Max's plan. Nor, as I had proved to my satisfaction, were the nurse and the chambermaid part of my police protection. I was in more deadly danger than ever, and I had walked into it almost of my own will. Apparently, having failed with the direct action of the cat burglar, the people back of the pepper-and-salt man were now using more subtle means. I wondered where they intended to kill me, and how.

I felt terribly cold, my hands so cold I kept them jammed into my pockets, but curiously enough, I no longer felt like a rat in a trap as I had while locked in that hotel room. Now that I was entirely on my own, it seemed to me my mind was much more active than usual. I pretended to be greatly interested in the scenery, the misty noon sight of London in the distance, the odd little sidelights of life in Richmond Town, and I kept exclaiming about everything I saw while I leaned forward as near as I could to the door handle without touching it and arousing their suspicions.

Nurse Tusingham tapped me on the shoulder. I looked around. She was not quite so eager and gossipy. I fancied just a trace of impatience flickering over her heavy-jawed face. "You talk a good deal, my girl, but you don't make much sense. Did you know that?"

"It's because I can't hear myself," I said apologetically. All the while, I was wondering how I could get out of this car without killing myself or getting killed on the way out by Nurse Tusingham or the tall, lean chauffeur.

The car lurched to a stop for cross-traffic in Richmond. All my senses were alert, except the important balancing sense I would have obtained from my hearing. For the first time I understood to the full just how much I had relied upon my ears to tell me where traffic was when I walked along busy streets. I had heretofore assumed that my eyes did the protective work, but it wasn't so at all. I must remember that when I escaped from the car.

Nurse Tusingham tapped my shoulder again. "Looking for someone, dearie?"

I shook my head and, looking back at her, said innocently, "If I'm to be kept in London—I believe it's called protective custody—I won't see much of these sweet little towns."

"Sweet little towns," the nurse repeated, rolling her bulbous eyes. "Well, hardly! Come and sit back, Miss Nona. If we stop suddenly again, you're liable to go clear through and land on Leecher's lap."

"Leecher?" I repeated, to be sure I understood, and then as Leecher turned around and looked at me, flashing a grin full of teeth, I was surprised at how well the unpleasant name suited him. In fact, his sharp profile was sharklike. I shivered as I thought of this cold-blooded creature with the teeth and the light like cold fire in his eyes as one of my intended executioners. But I hoped I was able to cover my reaction with a quick, flickering smile.

I sat back further on my seat but was careful to lean forward every few minutes to admire some building, street, or even the clothing of a passerby, anything I could think of in my desperate and panicky plan for escape. Searching for something innocuous to say, I ventured brightly, "Will Inspector MacLeish be sur-

prised that I came into town with you and didn't kick
and scream about it?"

The nurse raised her head and stared at me. Perhaps
she was wondering how any woman could be as naïve
and accept so unprotestingly this murderous kidnapping. I assume she decided I was stupid, for she
nodded and said something to Leecher that I couldn't
follow because of the rapid fluttering of her lips and
the chewing of her words. It nearly drove me crazy
wondering what she and Leecher said about me.

Just as my nerve was beginning to ooze out and my
confidence in my own agility reached bottom, I had
the terrific shock of seeing Max Brandt come out of a
shop on the now crowded sidewalk. In one respect the
sight raised my courage, and in another it jarred me to
the realization that I had to make my move now. There
might never be a better or even another time. I made
no move for an instant, hoping that I was the only one
in the car who had seen Max. I kept closely in mind
his direction and the buildings nearby. The car's speed
seemed to have picked up.

Then I pretended to admire a many-towered building on the far skyline through the windshield and
pointed at the tower, asking some inane question about
it just as the chauffeur swung the wheel over and
headed the car down a street to our right.

Just for that couple of seconds, Nurse Tusingham
and Leecher glanced off in the direction of the towered
structure as I saw that we were coming to a crowded
intersection that looked murky and indistinct in the
misty fog. I counted to five, still leaning forward with
the wide-eyed look of a typical first-time tourist. I did
not glance down, hoping to distract all attention from
my hand on the door handle.

Suddenly the moment came. The car jerked to a halt
on the left side of the street behind others in line as
cross-traffic again took over. I snapped the door handle
hard, propelled myself out into the street between cars
so fast and so hard that I went down on my knees, then

scrambled up, rushed to the sidewalk, and dodged madly around the corner. I did not once look back, and I was profoundly grateful to the early-afternoon fog, which seemed to swallow the world and me behind a misty, shimmering veil. I blessed the typical dress of English women in this climate; for ahead of me were two women wrapped, like me, in high-collared black coats, and no doubt, there were others behind me as well. If I had any kind of luck, my pursuers might mistake one of those women for me.

Between two narrow-faced buildings was an alleyway so small that I could barely get through it and, even then, had to make my way around a big barrel of trash. Slipping and sliding on the wet, broken cobbles, I was a little more than halfway through the alley, when I saw at the other end, like a floating horror in the mist, a woman in a white, stiff, nunlike coif, her nurse's habit covered by a uniform cape. I dodged behind another pile of trash and peered around it cautiously. The nurse who had paused at the alleyway was followed now by two others.

Deathly tired and a little sick to my stomach, I dropped behind a box full of cabbage leaves and potato peelings that smelled to high heaven and beyond. The abominable stench drove me on, barely in time. There were shadows from the other end of the alley and someone slipped. I heard nothing, but I could not mistake the oddly dancing shadow in the mist that I saw out of the corner of my eye.

I hurried out to the opposite street, after the three nurses, and then slowed until I passed them unobtrusively. I knew that I should report to a policeman, one of those competent, reasonably friendly bobbies I had seen in London, but the minute I did so, I would be whisked off to Inspector MacLeish and the "Hospital that I wouldn't fear."

If only I could find my way back to where I had seen Max on the street, all my troubles would be over!

It must be six or eight blocks from here. I knew only the general direction.

I started that way, back generally toward Richmond Hill, but trying to avoid being seen alone on the street. I walked either before or behind little groups until I passed the cross street a block from where I had escaped. I could not see the big black car up the street, so I assumed they had driven along the street up which I had escaped and were cruising about. In no time they would be back at this street, having squared the block. I crossed with a group of women shoppers and one or two men looking as if they did not belong with us. But they were all protection to me. I glanced back and suddenly saw the big black car roving down the street behind me, touring slowly, carefully. No doubt within that car Bertha Tusingham's bugged-out eyes and the shark face of the man called Leecher were eyeing everyone on the street, noting each woman dressed at all as I was.

I tried to make myself small and unobtrusive among the other passersby. Then I saw a chemist's shop and rushed inside. No one seemed to be about. The place looked like a strange, antiseptic laboratory in a movie about a mad scientist. I was very surprised. It was my first experience with what someone since has called "a real drugstore. The old-fashioned kind."

I backed as close against the odd bottles and mortars and pestles as possible in order not to be seen outside through the dingy window. While I stood, or crouched, in this compromising position, the chemist came in. He spoke to me, but I did not understand him, for he mumbled badly. I explained that I could not hear, but I didn't go into details. I asked him if he had anything for a bad cough, which was rather stupid, as I hadn't coughed once in the shop, but it was the first thing I could think of. He surprised me by having a modern box of something called "pastilles," which he sold to me. After asking if he could help me in any way, and being refused, he went about his work in the back somewhere. I waited as long as I could without being too suspicious-looking to the chemist; then I went to the door and looked out carefully. The same crowd seemed to be walking by. There was no black car in sight. I hurried out and walked up the street as fast as I could, feeling now the pull of the muscles in my legs and stopping every few minutes to rub my ankle or rest one foot. I had just stopped a second time against a bookshop window, with my back to the door of the shop, when I felt myself suddenly seized around the waist. I started to scream. Gloved hands clamped hard over my mouth, so hard that I could not even bite. My head seemed to burst with the pressure.

Chapter Seven

I FELT myself turned around roughly and was face to face with Max Brandt. When he was sure I would not scream, he took his hand away from my face.

"I could kill you!" I cried between fury and what I suspected might, at any minute, be a flood of nervous and frightened tears. "I was never so scared! You Orangeman, you!"

He laughed and, taking my arm, hurried me along in spite of my stumbling and complaints.

"I thought it was the police taking me to London," I explained breathlessly. "Your girlfriend, Nurse Tusingham, was running things. But I'm sure she's one of *them.*"

"Them?"

"Yes." And to get his sympathy for my silly behavior a minute ago, I added rather a low blow. "You remember. The ones who executed that girl you loved, the one who looked like me."

He was not laughing now. He was looking dour and a little frightening. I watched his lips carefully.

"Ilona was not executed by *them,* but by . . ."

"Yes?"

"By others. Come. We have no time. They mean to get you. And if they do not, someone in MacLeish's organization will."

This was a new horror. "Not Scotty's people!"

"There is a traitor. Someone he trusts. He hasn't found which. But I can't risk your being in their hands until we know of the identity of the ones who may be set to dispose of you."

I did nothing then but trot along, sometimes half-dragged, until we came to a little side street where an MG several years old was parked. Max, with his arm still around me, hustled me into the car.

Relieved as I was to be in his strong hands again, I could not help making a little joke. "This is the second time I have been kidnapped today. But this time, I rather like it."

He looked at me, settled me as comfortably as possible in the little car, then went around and got in. Before starting the car, he reached over me and gently turned up the collar of my coat, which had fallen down flat in my hurry and my panic. As his fingers moved away, they lingered briefly upon my cheek, and when I touched them with my lips, he leaned far over, cutting me off from the light, and kissed me. For that brief time I felt as if I were encompassed by darkness, but I was not yet frightened of him. I was too much infatuated with him for that.

We both must have known the immediacy of our varied dangers, but during that precious minute all of them were forgotten. Then he drew away and started the car, looking back innumerable times to see if we had been observed. I looked back too, but there was no black car in sight, only the usual traffic with many pedestrians dressed in that comfortable, bundled, easy way I had found indigenous to the section of England with which I was becoming more or less familiar.

We drove through town and out, not toward the open country, as I had expected, supposing we would cut across to London Airport. Instead, we drove into the monumental confusion of midafternoon traffic in the Outer London area. When we crossed the Thames, I pretended to be admiring all the buildings I had known for years through my schoolbooks, but I was beginning to wonder, to be a trifle uneasy over this ride, even aside from the dangers of pursuit. Not that I mistrusted Max, I told myself—not at all. But things were happening unexpectedly, one after another, and I could not understand them. If every move was explained to me, and the reasons for it, felt sure I could cope with anything. Since he was driving, and frequently checking the little rear-view mirror for any signs of our being followed, I could not talk to him, or rather, understand his answers. But presently, when we passed the Houses of Parliament, the Hotel Savoy, and later the Tower of London, and paused for traffic, I ventured, "Aren't we flying to the Continent? They're sure to trace your car if you go through all these highly populated areas, aren't they?"

He said with what, to me, was a frighteningly calm expression, "We can't make it today. Not in that direction."

I saw his hand upon the wheel. Despite his ease of expression, the knuckles of his fingers showed white with pressure, and whenever he glanced at the rear-view mirror, there was tension around his eyes. Being deprived of one sense, I seemed to use all the others much more carefully.

"Is it the ones who kidnapped me?" I asked, watching for the slightest sign from him. It was difficult to read his lips when we were traveling at this speed and through busy intersections.

"Our friend Scotty MacLeish is on the lookout for us at London Airport."

"How do you know?" I paused, then added when I realized, "But you had just come from there, across town, when I saw you on the street in Richmond."

He surprised me by contradicting me, "No. I was there earlier at London Airport. Since, I've been to three. I've driven since I left you this morning. MacLeish's men are everywhere. And where they aren't, the others are. Somehow, they must have suspected what we were up to." He slapped the wheel so hard that I jumped, startled by the gesture, if not by the sound. "How did they discover our plan? Are you sure you told no one?"

"Positive," I assured him abruptly, alarmed that it might be my fault. "I talked to no one." Then, hesitating, I spoke in what I hoped was a small, humble voice, since I thought that very likely this thing was due to some accidental indiscretion on my part. "Where —where are we going now? What can we do?"

We were out of London by this time, and he stopped the car at an intersection where a meandering little country lane from the west emptied into our big north-south highway. He looked over at me, smiling faintly, and reached for my hand. Not being able to judge his mood by this gesture which might be merely to quiet me, I studied his eyes, the lines in his face, the tension he could not conceal.

"*Liebchen,* trust me."

"I do. Of course I do." You always say that when asked. It is a bit of blarney that's expected in answer to such a remark. "But then, can you tell me where we are going?"

"To a place that will suit you admirably, sweetheart."

He slapped my hand in a playful way and started to turn the wheel. I was sure he intended to turn sharply left into the little westerly lane, but more or less automatically, he glanced up at the rear-view mirror, and then the car shot forward, northward at a great speed. I twisted around and looked back. Several cars and a truck were following us.

"Which of them is it?" I asked, feeling breathless, aware of a painful constriction at my chest.

"The lorry."

"You mean the truck? How do you know? You can't see their faces."

"I know the lorry. It has been used before."

I subsided, crouching down in my seat, not looking at Max. How could Max know all these things? And had it been the police he saw, or the mysterious *them?*

"Don't be afraid," Max said calmly, obviously observing my actions without appearing to. "It won't be the first time this little motor has purred off to beat that lorry."

"Shouldn't we stop and get help from the police? I mean—it's better than being killed by those people."

He shook his head. It was all I could do, at the speed we were traveling, to get the full impact when he said with a spare motion of his lips, "One of *them* is with Scotty's men, as I said." And when I caught my breath at the pincers in which we appeared to be trapped, he added, "We don't dare fall into the hands of that person, whoever he may be."

I covered my face and tried to make myself as small as possible. In all my life, I had never felt so helpless. I was not brought up to be beholden to others, even a man I loved—or with whom I was infatuated. I was sure I loved him, in an obvious, physical way. Why, then, had I felt this strange, creeping fear during the last few minutes? Fear in which Max had a part. He knew too much. I told myself this as my excuse for the beginnings of these thoughts, which were so treacherous that I was ashamed to acknowledge them.

"It's perfectly dreadful." I complained, raising up after a few minutes and looking back. "Does Scotty actually know that one of the men he trusts is with the other side?"

"He certainly suspects. He is not stupid. But it requires a bit more than suspicion. Probably, he doesn't want to jeopardize his relationships with any of the foreign agents who are worth so much to him."

"Like you. How horrible! What a monster he must be, the creature who is betraying Scotty and the others!"

"And what makes you think it is a man?"

I subsided, making bets with myself that the guilty party was Nurse Tusingham. When I considered her, it seemed to me that I had never seen anyone more evil, including that awful cat man. I was able to breathe freely for the first time since seeing the big green lorry, when Max turned at another of those country lanes, and we rattled along, soon swallowed up fore and aft by richly green hedges, whose presence I considered a remarkable piece of luck. I remarked upon this luck.

"No," said Max. "I counted on them."

No doubt, I thought, they had served him before. This journey whose inception had been so romantic was beginning to appear a routine matter, something Max had done before. I wondered if his previous companions had been women.

I sat stiffly in my seat, very near the door, for some time before I realized how I must look to my companion, as though I wanted to get as far away from him as possible. We had driven out of the mist and fog of London weather, and the long rays of the afternoon brightened noticeably, like a pale lady suddenly rouged. At one of the many curves in the hedge-lined road was one of those country inns I've heard about all my life and seen often in movies, a romantic little half-timbered place with a thatched roof and charming little leaded windows. To complete the picture the front door was open invitingly, and inside it looked dark but glowing with warmth and with wonderfully appetizing smells that seemed to be both ham and bacon.

We had been driving as fast as the bumpy, twisting lane would let us, and neither of us said much. Once he asked me to get out a map of the midlands, which I happened to be sitting on, and I read off the side roads through the peculiar countryside called Wiltshire and approaching the borders of Somerset. I had thought this area would be full of quaint towns, English roses, and romantic, meandering streams, but we must have come across quite another section, because until we saw that little inn, we had seemed cut off from humanity, nothing in sight but more and more bleak downs, where sheep roamed but no sheepcotes were visible, where there were hedgerows now and then, but no houses, no people. I remember thinking it was the first time in my life I had ever been so far from the civilization I had grown up with. And then, I thought of Max and curled up a little more with shame at all my treacherous thoughts about the stranger I was about to marry. I looked longingly at the inn we were approaching, and Max must have seen my expression and guessed my feelings. It did not make my conscience about him clearer to see how attentive he was to my moods.

"You look a little tired, Nona. Shall we stop? It's rather like a pub, but you won't mind that. The beer and ale should be excellent." As he stopped the car in front of the inn, he tried to make a little joke, on a subject that no longer seemed amusingly romantic to me. "You must acquire a taste for beer, *Liebchen*. It is the only possible drink to take with red cabbage and potato pancakes. And you do remember your promise."

I smiled weakly, pulling myself together so that when he came around and got me out of the little car, I was able to appear pleased. But the truth is, though we had come a long way from London, I still did not know where we were going or how Max expected to get the two of us out of the country. He had evaded my one or two questions like an adult pacifying a child, and I hadn't wanted to pursue it when I didn't yet know quite what my feelings were about him.

As we walked across the mossy path to the door, I looked quickly up and down the road. Nothing was in sight except some kind of stone figure, like an obelisque, I thought, but as we stepped up on higher ground at the inn door I saw that it was only one stone on spreading fields full of such strange monuments and pagan-looking crosses. They seemed to enclose the inn on three sides, imprisoning the pretty little huddled building.

"We've thrown them off for the moment," Max said. "Don't worry."

"I wasn't. I just realized that is a graveyard."

He laughed as if surprised at my remark. "Nona, little one, don't tell me you are superstitious."

I shuddered. "Horribly. It's a bad omen. Terribly bad luck."

"You Irish," he remarked, but more in amusement than disgust, I thought. By such tiny means—a little smile, a quirk of his powerful, ugly mouth, an ever so slight movement toward me of his hard hands—my pulses beat faster. I loved him in this way, but I did not know how many other ways I loved him, because in my mind, I was beginning to distrust and even fear him. This, however, did not prevent my holding to his arm, thankful for the strength beneath my fingers, wondering that a man of his worldly experience and his mysterious political past should seem to care genuinely about me.

We entered by a dark little passage that did not lighten perceptibly as we moved to one side. We did not, as I had expected, go into the dining room and bar, but to the other side, which was called the common room in books I had read. It was a delightfully informal sitting room with a huge, soot-scarred fireplace now sparkling and (I've no doubt) snapping with something like coal that turned out to be peat. From the way he had teased me, I expected Max to order beer or ale for himself, but instead he drank Burgundy and said the Burgundy here was the best in the West Country. There were all the succulent little foods I had got used to in England at teatime. I liked the patés, the very odd but tasty Scotch eggs, and best of all the gingerbread. I had been too nervous to eat breakfast, I had missed lunch, and now it was amazing how my courage returned when my appetite was satisfied. Max deliberately sat in the mottled light so I could read his lips and we could talk. I carefully avoided asking questions about the marriage we had planned. I knew now that I did not want to rush into anything that involved my whole lifetime. I wanted to know Max better, to feel less unnerved in his presence, and above all, to be quite sure that Max wasn't still a part, even a small part, of the evil that threatened to engulf me.

For this reason, Max's next words made me tense with dread. He leaned forward from his chair and stole a few crumbs of my gingerbread. "You have not asked me about the license or why we haven't visited a registry office. Aren't you worried for fear I am seducing you? Carrying you off to some fate worse than death?"

I laughed at the idea—and then, while I was watching him speak, I saw a shadow cross outside the window behind him, one of those faint streaks blotting the light momentarily which often prove to be no more than a flicker of the eyelid. Nevertheless, it startled me so much that I exclaimed something and jumped up, pointing toward the little, squared panes of the window. I half-expected him to laugh or scowl at my absurd fright, but he swung around with his hand in the patch pocket of the worn black topcoat that hung from his shoulders now that we were inside the warm room. He asked me something quickly and took long steps toward the window.

"I don't know what it is. Probably nothing," I said, overturning my chair in my anxiety to keep from letting my back become a target. It was the silence, I think, that consciousness of things creeping up on me without my knowing they were there, that added to my fright. I don't know why the element of surprise made my danger so much more horrible.

He must have seen at once that there wasn't anything at the window, but he kept his coat hung over one shoulder, with one hand still buried in the pocket. I tried, without being obvious about it, to see if the thing in his pocket was a gun. The thought made me shiver. If I should decide not to go further, or to go off on my own, would he use that gun on me? Probably not. But I couldn't be sure. The doubt did not reassure me.

"Do you see anything?" I asked in a quavering voice whose weakness I was ashamed of.

He turned to me briefly. "Nothing but the graveyard. You were right. It is everywhere. Depressing thought." He raised the latch and looked out over the tombstones and then to the right and left.

I stayed where I was, ready to run.

He relocked the window and came back across the room. He appeared much more casual now. I had a feeling that when the waiter-landlord appeared, as he did immediately, brought by my loud outburst, I became safe, protected, since *he* could not possibly have any reason to kill me. Or could he? My thoughts were in turmoil again. But humanity was here in the room now. I was not alone with an unknown quantity.

"Will you be staying over, mum . . . sor?"

I was in the midst of saying, "We'll be going," when Max came back to his chair.

"It will be dark in another hour," he suggested. "What do you say we stay here a little while so you may get some rest?"

I glanced at the red-haired, blunt-nosed innkeeper and saw that he was looking curiously at Max. While Max was adding reasons for remaining at the inn so that we could travel after dark instead, the innkeeper went over to the window and opened it. He looked out. I watched him carefully.

"Jem, what'll you be doing hereabouts? Off! Be off now, will you?" The innkeeper turned from one to the other of us. "He's a poor idjut. Means you no harm. Did he set you afright, mum?"

I started up again in new terror, glancing at Max. "You said there was no one out there."

Max replied to me patiently, seeming unruffled by the implication of mistrust in my words, "No one was out there a minute ago." And then, taking my wrist, he said, "Come along. I want to talk to you, Nona."

Though I could not hear his voice, I recognized the manner behind the tone, and I obeyed. He led me out through the little entrance passage that was cool, damp, and dark. We went up a twisted staircase. All this time I was remembering that he very likely had a gun in his topcoat pocket, and there was no question about his superior strength, even without it. Even so, from the first moment when I had woke up that morning after being deafened, I had known that Max Brandt's greatest influence over me was not his physical strength but the sensual or sensuous attraction he held for me.

The room he took me to was warm and quaint, with a low beamed ceiling. It was a bedroom with one large, ostentatious four-poster bed, which dominated the old-fashioned room. I did not do more than glance at it and then look quickly away.

"Excellent for the purpose of giving madame a little rest," said Max, adding to the innkeeper, "Have my car taken around to the back of the inn immediately." He gave the man some coins.

We were alone then.

"I think you ought to know," I said stiffly, "that I've changed my—"

"Be quiet!" He cut me short. "I don't suppose you got a good look at the idiot hanging about in the cemetery."

I shook my head.

"You're sure? He looked very like someone I've seen in London . . . or at Richmond. . . . Well, no matter. We'll soon know."

I wet my lips, made an effort, and asked, "You think they got here ahead of us? How could they know? From your license, I suppose. Do you think he's one of Scotty's men or one of the . . . others?"

"It can't matter which, if it should be the traitor."

"Don't!"

He motioned me to the bed and walking more or less backward, I obeyed until I leaned back against the faded patchwork coverlet. "I am going to see what those fellows are up to, but I'd rather they didn't know it." He stopped and looked penetratingly into my face. "My poor *Liebchen,* you look so very tired. Please try and rest, for my sake."

"Don't—" I wanted to say, "Don't betray me to them but I couldn't get the words out. I pretended to obey him, feeling the high bed behind me as a barrier beyond which I could not retreat.

He misunderstood my concern. "Don't worry. I'll

take care. Do as I say now. Promise?" He smiled, almost a gentle smile. "Good. When I return, I see we shall need a little talk about the future. Don't you agree?"

I agreed numbly, and he left the room, motioning to me to lock it after him. It was a fine, cautious command but impossible to fulfill. There was no lock on the door, only a flimsy latch, which might be raised by a bobby pin. I examined it, wondering how such a door and latch could be made secure.

I need not worry now, I told myself, so long as Max was with me, except for that other and more harrowing suspicion, that Max himself knew too much about flight and had managed to instill me with fears almost equally of Scotty's men and of the mysterious Other Side, which I assumed to be Communists.

There was nothing I could think of to do to this flimsy latch now, and in any case, a barricade would be difficult to explain to Max when he returned. I went over to the window and looked out. This was the other side of the inn, and a part of the graveyard extended from the east and north to end almost opposite my window. The stones would have been fascinating if I had not been on edge from thinking of the death I had escaped this morning when I leaped out of that black car. Papa and Mother had many pictures of the old Gaelic crosses in graveyards near their childhood coteens in Ireland, so I was not surprised to see several that rather suggested the Gaelic cross.

Suddenly, the late-afternoon sun cast two shadows that lengthened as two men came into view from the back of the inn. I ducked behind the curtains and continued to look out, thinking one of them must be the landlord who had driven Max's car out of sight of the highway. It was not, though. One of the men was blond, slouching, round-shouldered, and wearing a worn, stained old jacket that did not fit him. This must be the feeble-minded man the landlord had mentioned. Then I saw the other. It was Max, and he was talking

with the supposed idiot volubly, waving his hand in the
European way to emphasize.

Surely, I thought, staring at the two men, the "idiot"
looked more square-shouldered now, intelligent and
knowing, as the two men gazed up at my window, not
seeing me behind the curtains.

So that was it! They knew each other. And they were
discussing me. There still might be a perfectly logical
explanation. I would have to wait and see what Max
said. As the two men parted, the supposedly feeble-
minded man going back through the gravestones and
Max coming toward the inn, I recalled very distinctly
that he had not seen the idiot beyond that window
downstairs, whereas the landlord had seen him. It was
possible Max really hadn't seen him. On the other
hand, if he had lied, there must be powerful reasons.
I felt fairly sure my own fate was the most powerful of
those reasons. Had they been discussing it just a moment ago, below my window?

"Let's see if he denies talking to the fellow," I said
to myself, "as he denied seeing him earlier." One way
or another, I could be fairly sure what to expect then.

Chapter Eight

THE MINUTES until Max returned seemed very long. After a little thought I opened the door as quietly as I could, praying that I would soon either get my hearing back or learn to do things as soundlessly as this new world of silence did things around me. I went out on the dark landing, carefully feeling my way, took hold of the rickety banister, and looked down at the entrance passage of the inn directly below.

What a time to be so stupidly deaf! If I could only hear, I might at least know what these people were up to without being seen. It had never before occurred to me that the handicap of deafness, even though temporary, as Max and the other doctors said, still made it impossible really to know a person without the mask all people assume in the presence of another. Eavesdropping could be so educational. It might even save my life. I looked downward, hoping to learn something in that dim little area below the stairs. It was too dark to read anyone's lips, but I thought it might be possible to get an idea of Max's mood and manner when not in my company. That might reveal something about his sincerity toward me, even his motives.

Max came in alone a few minutes later, after I had become cramped and tired and was sitting on the top stair, hugging my knees and peering cautiously between the banister posts. I saw him stop inside the door and call someone who proved to be a very pretty brunet girl with a catalog of figure advantages, but her figure being short, I thought these advantages were just a little closer together than they might have been. They were successful enough, however, to give her the con-

fidence I had always envied in such women. And worst
of all, Max seemed very friendly with her. I nearly
died of curiosity, wondering what he really said to her,
whether he cared about her and her flirtatious little
chatter. She kept fingering the shoulder of his coat, and
I imagined she might be working around toward getting
at the weapon I suspected was in his pocket. On the
other hand, she might merely be trying for an affair and
hoping to excite him. I, in my hidden place, hoped
desperately that she would fail, that he would not be
moved.

They discussed something that involved a good many
gestures toward the interior of the inn on the ground
floor and then up toward where I was crouched in the
dark. I ducked back to be sure I was not seen by either
of them. They agreed on something. She patted him on
the back of the hand while I, in the dark of the staircase, burned in solitary jealousy. It was odd, I thought
even then, that I could be jealous concerning Max
when I wasn't even sure he was on my side in this
flight of ours.

Before I realized what had happened they walked a
few steps to the foot of the stairs, where the girl hustled away and Max started up the stairs. I, above the
stair landing, scrambled to get up and hurry inside our
room. It was too late, however. I was horrified to find
that the toes of one foot were asleep and I couldn't get
up at my first attempt. I managed to crinkle my toes up
and was just jumping up, when Max reached me. He
nearly stepped on me but saw me just in time and called
my name in what I'm sure must have been astonishment before he reached down, took my elbow, and
lifted me to my feet.

"I got lonesome," I lied swiftly, "and I came out to
see where you had gone. Is there anything suspicious
going on?"

"Suspicious! Of course not. What could be suspicious in a quiet little place like this? You're trembling. I've no doubt you've a temperature as well." He

ushered me into the room assigned to us. "Come along. You should be resting, not rushing about like this." He looked into my face, and then, seeing my humiliation and the residue of the old fear, he made the mistake of assuming they were due to fever. I did not try to change his mind but let him lead me across the room, which was gaudily lighted by the sunset over the rolling downs.

The bed looked very high, and I made an effort to climb up with one knee, but slipped off and murmured, "I'm all right. Honestly. It's just that I'm tired and scared—that is . . . tired."

"I understand." He reached for me, and the minute he touched me, I started to struggle. You would have thought I was being savagely skinned, at the very least. Suddenly, he had tight hold of my shoulders and was so close that I saw the flecks of light in his deep-set dark eyes. "Look at me, *Liebchen*. And believe me. When you wish me to love you, I shall. Now, you are too tired. You understand what I am saying?"

"Yes, yes. Certainly." He must think I was an infant. But I was too tired and secretly worried to argue.

"Good." Then, as I stiffened with a premonition of my own weakness, he suddenly lifted me high up off the floor, and I was in his arms, aware of his pulse, his warmth, and his strength. He held me while I might have counted five. Then he dropped me gently on the bed and plumped up the pillows behind me.

The stitching that joined the patches of the coverlet was rough under my body. I thought I was too tired or nervous to rest, and apparently Max understood this. He had leaned over me to arrange the pillows. Now he took a step or two back and then perched himself on the foot of the bed and watched me, with a teasing smile not nearly so sophisticated and cynical as the cast of his countenance suggested.

"You can't sleep this early, I suppose."

"No. It's all the danger—the things that have piled

on top of each other. I just can't . . ." There were no words. But he seemed to know, all the same.

"I understand. Well then, if you would feel better in talking, I will listen. I will even answer, whatever makes you rest and feel reassured."

I looked at the beamed ceiling, saw a cobweb dangling, and thought this place must have few visitors. It was the ideal scene to hide out—or to murder a person who was hiding out.

"May I ask one question, Max?"

"One? Very well. I promise to answer one. It should be very special. What do you wish to know? My salary? If I love a certain surprising young person? Ask."

I sat up, leaning on my elbows.

"Who was Ilona?"

He reacted faintly but with that peculiar white tension which went even to his lips. "Who?"

"Ilona. The girl who looked like me. Who was she?"

He closed his eyes, a gesture that was short and swift as a wink. "My wife. We were married in Dresden nineteen forty-four. We were very young and idealistic."

I winced at the name of the elegant, enchanting old city whose splendor was gone forever.

"Was she killed in the fire raids? I've read about them. It was horrible."

He smiled, but this time cynically. "All raids are horrible. I was doing work for the British and Americans at the time. That made it a little more horrible, since, in some respects, I was to blame for the raids. Ilona was not in Dresden itself during the fire raid, but she never forgave them. Later, she . . . died."

"I'm so sorry. I shouldn't have brought it all back to you like this."

He sat there looking at me as the sun went down and his face was thrown into shadow. "You have brought it back to me every minute of every day since I first saw you. It was nothing anyone could avoid. You were just . . . before me. Before my eyes, even when I was away from you. . . . You wouldn't know what I am talking about, and I can't explain."

For me it was an emotional as well as mental strain, leaning forward to understand his words. He did not often speak so much without pauses to see that I understood. Perhaps he was sincere in this. I felt that he meant very deeply all he said about the dead Ilona. It was quite possible that he had saved my life only because I reminded him of the dead woman. Surely I had been wrong in my suspicions of him! Even without hearing his voice, I guessed the depths of emotion behind this bitter memory he related to me.

Still, though, I felt I had lulled away the alertness, the careful, warning note that would prepare him with an alibi when I asked him that special question. I was preparing the right disarming words when he said abruptly, "What are you thinking?"

"Thinking? I wasn't really. I was only—"

"You were thinking. You should not think. You should be resting."

I pretended to close my eyes, all obedience, but I was watching him as I murmured sleepily, "You were gone a long time. Did you see anyone suspicious?"

"Not a soul. This isn't resting. You are not to worry. If you wish to have your hearing return, you are going to have to be calm, to get much rest."

"No. Really. Did you meet anyone outside in that awful graveyard?"

"Certainly not. What should I meet in a graveyard? Ghosts of the dead?"

So there ·had been something suspicious in his secretive conversation with the feeble-minded man! And I had just begun to feel better about him, aware once more of all the irresistible qualities in him that had first attracted me. It was no use. I would have to leave him and strike out on my own, trusting to luck and whatever skill at dodging pursuit that I had learned from him. It was a sickening thing to find my faith in him undergoing these terrible ups and downs.

The bed shivered under me as if struck by an earthquake. My eyes snapped open, and I found myself staring at his frowning, forbidding face.

"Don't pretend with me, Nona! You are not sleepy. You are not in pain. Why were you pretending?"

"I don't know what you mean. Pretending! Do I have to be pretending every time my eyes are closed?"

He looked at me steadily, in silence for a few seconds. "Your eyes were not closed."

I knew he could not tell this merely by looking at me, and I gave myself away by tacit admission when I asked with keen curiosity, "How did you know?"

"Because you went right on exchanging conversation with me. You could not have done that if your eyes were closed."

It was a stupid mistake, the kind of stupid mistake that might cost a person in my dangerous spot her life. I must remember details like this. I must be exceedingly careful and remember.

"Thank you, Max," I said softly, the irony hidden, I hoped.

In spite of his now puzzled air, he had to smile a little. "For what? My rudeness?"

"No. For reminding me."

That gave him plenty to think about. He was still puzzling it out when I pursued the question of his mysterious stroll "alone" around the inn, through that graveyard.

"Was there really an idiot out in that awful graveyard, as the landlord said? He sounds a little dangerous. He could be working for those killers, couldn't he?"

"My dear child, *they* do not employ idiots, let me assure you on that score." He took up my wrist between thumb and forefinger, apparently to take my pulse, and glanced at the watch on his other hand.

Suddenly, he dropped my hand as if startled, and looked quickly across the room. Something furtive and startled in his expression alarmed me more than his gesture. He must have heard someone at the door. The panic inside me surged up at the same time as I realized again the thousand ways that death could strike at my back while I knew nothing of its approach. I had not even the peculiar sense of danger that so many other handicapped people seemed to develop for their protection.

Max looked at me, touched his finger to his lips significantly, and went to the door. He threw it open abruptly, but even I could see that beyond him there was nothing, only the shadowy stair landing. He turned back to me and motioned for me to put a chair against the door when he had gone. He took several steps toward me.

"When I return, I will push open the door an inch or two. You will see this." He pointed to the heavy, foreign-looking old signet ring he wore on the third finger of his left hand. I nodded, understanding this precaution which got around the problem of my holding him off by mistake for the others when he returned. Then he went out and closed the door, and I, getting off the bed, went and followed his directions carefully. I tucked a chair back under the latch and stuffed one of my pillows under the door, to make it more difficult to push open. I was perfectly aware that anyone could get in with a bit of good, stiff exertion, but if it proved to be someone else, not Max, I could make life miserable for him and even, by a few lusty hits with the remaining chair in the room, could break the intruder's arm. Or better yet, I thought, break his head. Papa was always blarneying about the wicked Black-and-Tans whose heads he had broken during the Troubles in Ireland. And I was not above repeating the act, if necessary.

I listened against the door for a while, pretending I could hear sounds, creaking stairs, the distant murmur of voices; but throughout it there was the incessant roar that drowned it all, and I knew that these faint signs of what I took to be returning sounds were imaginary. I went over to the window and looked out. I was surprised to see a half-moon hanging low in the night-blue sky. I hadn't realized it was so late. After the brightness of the sky, the ground seemed doubly forbidding, sprinkled as it was with those enormous and ancient gravestones. The Gaelic markers in particular looked like huge, faceless creatures in cassocks, with arms in deep sleeves outstretched, cruciform. I opened the window and looked out in each direction. There was not a soul in sight, but that wasn't surprising. Not many people would be likely to wander about graveyards after dark. It was, come to think of it, a very odd place for a graveyard, or for an inn connected to it.

I supposed that, as was often the case, the inn had formerly been a church property and had for some reason been turned into a public inn in times past.

In the distance, however, where the moon hung close above the horizon, were rolling hills, treeless and bleak, seeming without end. I found myself depressed, hoping every minute that Max would return in the next. He did not, though.

I gave him ten minutes more, then stretched a point and gave him half an hour. I pictured him going downstairs, answering whatever summons had brought him to the door and down the dark flight of stairs. There would be a discussion, perhaps, and . . .

On the other hand, suppose no one had summoned him. Suppose he had heard something. Now, I was getting close to the logical happening. . . . His behavior suggested that he had gone off to find who was prowling around our room. And the longer he was delayed in returning, the more I conjured up horrors to him.

A dozen times I looked out the window. When more than an hour had passed, I saw squares of light pour out across the graveyard from the windows of the attic above my head, where the servants probably slept. Otherwise, the whole building seemed to be as deserted as its silence to me would indicate. I found myself alone here with nothing but the dead.

When the evening wore on and the silence became

more than usually unbearable, I could not stand the suspense of this self-imprisonment any longer. I went over to the door and carefully removed the barricade. I peeked out and was surprised and reassured to see a plain, low-wattage lightbulb that cast the stairs in striped shadow through the banisters and dropped a little pool of light on the entrance passage. As I watched I was relieved to see the red-haired landlord laying down orders to the shapely young woman in some domestic crisis or other. They crossed the pool of light and went toward what I guessed must be the kitchen.

There was still no sign of Max, but at least I wasn't entirely alone. And where on earth was Max? Had he deserted me completely? It is strange as I think of it now, but although I had at moments suspected Max Brandt of many things, I never believed he would simply walk out and leave me in this place where I knew no one and where he knew I suspected everyone.

I sneaked down the stairs, huddled against the wall that smelled of ancient, dry timbers and dust, until I was in the passageway where I nearly walked into a tousled, friendly-looking boy about twelve who was carrying a bucket of slops. He asked me something, blinking eyes with sandy lashes, and I shook my head, telling him I could not hear. He did not seem to think this anything out of the way, but when I asked him if he had seen Max, and I described him, the boy mouthed words so carefully that I could not mistake what he said.

"I never seen un, mum. Not about here, I ain't."

"No," I said. "You misunderstood me. Doctor Brandt has been here for some hours. We arrived together. I am his patient. But he really is in the building. I know that."

"But mum," the boy protested, waving the slop bucket for emphasis, while I ducked out of its way. "I been in ever' room in the place. I been dumpin' slops.

It's our off-time for the tours. There's no doctor like you say. Not in this bit of a place for haunts."

I began to walk around, looking into odd corners. It was curious that no visitors were here at all. No casual travelers stopping for an ale or a gin and bitters, no one spending the night. . . . I could not hear the traffic noises out on the room, of course, so I went to the big, ages-old front door and started to open it to look out. The door was surprisingly heavy, and the boy set down his bucket of slops to help me.

"You lookin' for some'ut, mum?" he asked me, as though he had not heard a word I said.

"For the doctor. I know he is here."

The boy shook his head, and I lost my temper and said loudly, "You're very impudent. You know perfectly well Doctor Brandt is in this building, or else he has been somewhere on the grounds. He and I sat in that room having cocktails and a snack several hours ago."

"No'm," said the boy. "Boss says—Boss, that's him as own the place—Yank talk, you know. He says nobody's been here to stay exceptin' the pretty lady. That'll be you."

Chapter Nine

I WOULD have preferred his having sighted Max to all the compliments in the world.

"Never mind that. What is your name? Who are you? Do you live here with your people?"

"Name's Tod Humber, mum. I'm here in service to my uncle. That's the gent with the reddish hair. They call me Toddles. Sort of a friendly name, as you might say."

All of which had nothing to do with me, I thought. "And how long is it since you came on duty, Toddles?"

"Teatime. That'll be it. Hard on teatime. It was when the London folk spilled the tea on the cozy and the pot was sizzling. What a cleanup that was, you may be sure."

I closed the partially opened street door and stared at him very hard. "Ted—Tod, that is, who were these London folks? Do you know them? Have you ever seen or served them before?"

"Not the lady, no. A bad business it is, too. They never gave me tuppence for all the mopping up I did. And she spoke bad, too. Real Billingsgate, like they say." He scratched his head and then added fairly, "But for all that, she was a looker. That she was."

I began to think that in questioning him I had gone off on a wild-goose chase. Hundreds of travelers must take this road from London to the West Counties every day. There was nothing significant about these few visitors. Conspirators would hardly arrive at this out-of-the-way inn in pursuit of Max and me, complete with a noticeably pretty woman. It would hardly be a very shrewd act to include such a conspicuous aid to

94

murder. And if it were Scotty's government people, it was even more unlikely that they would have included a pretty, flashy woman.

"Well then, can you help me to look around the inn? Outside, I mean. I'm sure Doctor Brandt has gone out there to—to put his car away. And to investigate."

"What'll he be investigatin', mum? There's no ruins hereabouts. They'll be over the downs yon. They're a funny sort entirely. You like all them places what's been lived in back in olden days? Real olden days, that is. Cave days."

"No. I don't particularly like it." I was not in the mood to think of weird prehistoric ruins, with their ghostly moonlight shadows, at a time like this. "But the truth is, Doctor Brandt was here, and he is not here now." I opened the door and looked out. Almost at that moment a British car whizzed past and disappeared around the next curve in the little road. I devoutly wished I was in that car. If, that is, I could be sure Max was safe.

Tod took his slop bucket and started away rather hesitantly, looking back at me. "If you've a mind to, you can come with me. Then you can look about you. If you like, you can stand on one of the flat stones in the graveyard and get a real good look at the place in the distance where the old ones lived long ago."

I saw it was no use my telling him I wasn't a historian. Probably, everyone who stopped here headed for the ruins of the cave dwellers or whatever they were. On that night I was still happily ignorant of places like Stonehenge, Roman walls, Druid ruins, and what Papa referred to as "that ilk." A liberal and, if I may say so, a haunting education on that subject has only made me so susceptible that I get a ghostly shiver now when anyone points out a ruin over ten years old.

I went along with the boy, noticing that there were lights on the back of the inn, and I asked Tod about it as we were about to step out into the innyard through a side door.

"They were doin' up dishes. It's a bit odd, that. It's my job, usual. But they shooed me out."

"Why?"

Tod shrugged. "Town folks stay in the lounge by the fire, usual. But these two was in the kitchen as if they owned it. And they give Uncle Jolyon orders like he was me or some'ut."

"Are they there now?"

He gestured to me, and we stepped out and down two steps to the ground. Carefully, he closed the door behind him. The loose old doorknob was a high reach for him, but he would not let me touch it.

"Too much noise. There's a trick to closing it," he explained, stepping into the moonlight so that I might read his lips. I failed to understand anything he said the first time, except the necessity for quiet, but it all seemed clear when he threw out the slops in the most careless way and then set down the bucket and tiptoed along the house wall to where the light from the kitchen splashed out in front of us.

We both peered over the windowsill, Tod hopping on tiptoe, but although there were four teacups on the scratchy old wooden chopping table, plus a tea cozy drying on the big old-fashioned coal stove, the only person in the room was the pretty, curvacious brunet I had seen earlier. She was busy reading a tight-printed tissue-thin newspaper while she wiped three saucers at once.

"She's Pam Wattersley," Tod told me with strong disapproval. "Uncle's been and acted cross as sticks since she come." He wrinkled his freckled nose. "He likes her. Think of that. And her from London where the swells is. Like them others that come today. The yellow-haired female and the man."

Suddenly aware of a frightening possibility, I whispered, "Did you say London?"

"Well, Richmond. That's the same thing. As near as can be, Pam says."

I was right. I wished to heaven I wasn't. I pulled

Tod away from the window and retreated with him until I found the high heels of my shoes sinking in unnaturally soft ground. I had blundered into the graveyard. However, it seemed the most private place in which to enlist young Tod's help.

"Toddles, this is terribly important. Where is Doctor Brandt's MG?"

"So help me, mum, I been all around the inn. There's no MG. Even the folks from London is gone. Anyway, their car is gone too."

"Then we must look for tracks where the MG was parked."

"I dunno. . . . Good thing there's a moon."

He was a vigorous, clever boy, and presently on the other side of the inn near an old, empty barn, we saw tire marks that he guaranteed were made by an MG. I myself wouldn't have known the MG marks from those of a Rolls, but Tod seemed positive, and when I was convinced, I knew I could not wait longer.

"I'm in great danger. You must help me. These friends of your Miss Wattersley, they want to kill me." His eyes got very big and round, though when I added the words about Max, I could see he wasn't quite so sure of me. "They seem to have made away with my doctor, Max Brandt. It is his car, the MG, that we have been looking for."

"You'll be tellin' me its gangsters that's got this doctor chap?"

"A form of gangster, yes. Toddles, I have to get away. Any minute they may—"

"Oh, look!" Tod pointed at a new patch of light on the graveyard. "Someone's come into your room."

I huddled against the wall, beckoning to the boy and whispering, "See if you can find out if it's the man or woman from Richmond. Or if it's a dark man with heavy features."

"That's your doctor? I'll go. Will it be the police you go to after I've found out?"

"Yes. Run. Find out. It really is a matter of life and death."

"Just like on the flicks—life and death and all."

I remained very close to the inn's walls, following as silently as I could while the boy, galvanized by all this talk of life and death rushed around the house. Opposite the window of the room assigned to me he stepped well back into the graveyard so he could better see whoever had come into my room. When I reached him he spoke to me carefully. "It's the man and the yellow-haired lady. They be looking out for you, mark me."

I didn't doubt it. I remained in the shadows behind a weird but protective Gaelic cross and felt in my coat pockets. Of course, there was no money, only a green scarf for my head and a large black button I had pulled off my coat in the hope that I would remember to buy a sewing kit and sew it back on.

"Toddles, do you think you could be clever enough to get upstairs into my room and bring me my handbag?"

His eyes gleamed, and he was about to rush through the graveyard to carry out his dangerous mission, when he had a second thought. "Will you be telling me the truth of it, mum? You're not one of the gangsters now, be you? I mean—they're called a 'moll'—the ladies what's in with the gangsters."

I could not read his lips on that word "moll"; I could only guess at it and assure him that I was nobody's moll and that his uncle's friend, Pam Wattersley, had some mighty unsavory friends and associates.

"Is it true then, mum? You're fleeing for your life, like on the films?"

"Believe me, I am! I give you my most solemn word I am. Please hurry!"

"Aye." And he was off and running but skidded to a stop as I whispered, "Don't let them catch you. And whatever you do, don't tell them where I am. It's for" —I thought Papa must forgive me, and I said—"it's for England."

He made a solemn bob with his tousled head and dashed off again. I felt for the first time since Max had left me that I could count on someone for help.

Meanwhile, I remained in the deep shadow of the Gaelic cross and watched my window high above me. While I stood there, carefully hidden, my heart behaved oddly, and the fingers of each hand laced and unlaced with the fingers of the other. Sooner even than I would have expected, I saw Tod's wiry young form pass the window. He was talking to someone inside the room, or at the very least, he was gesticulating as if he talked to someone. Since my loss of hearing, I had been surprised to notice how much hand and arm and finger motion seemed necessary to punctuate people's speech.

Tod came to the window and looked down, almost directly at me. Then he gazed back over his shoulder and spoke to whoever was in my room. I held my breath. I expected any second to be pointed out to one of my enemies by Tod, who had turned traitor. No one else came, though, and Tod left the window. I thought of running, but I didn't know where to run without my flight being cut off by one of *them*. If only I could have counted on the boy! Or at the very least, if I could have had time and opportunity to call Scotty MacLeish!

When a swift-moving shadow cut across the first splash of light on the ground, I started to run across the far corner of the graveyard. Finding a hedge in my way, I followed it to its opening and got through. Almost immediately something sharp and small struck my shoulder, but aside from a slight sting, it left no mark, no blood or scratch. I jerked to a stop momentarily, and a small hand seized my arm. It was too dark for me to read Tod's assurance to me, but when he took a handful of objects out of a huge and dirty handkerchief and offered them to me, I understood that he had emptied my handbag for some reason and was offering me the contents.

"The telephone," I suggested. "Is it possible to use

one of the telephones in the house and call long distance?" He didn't know what *long distance* meant, and I amended it to, "Can you make a trunk call to London?" I realized it would require much less complication if I had Tod call Richmond and leave a number where we might wait for Scotty in some nearby village.

But it was no use. Tod shook his head. He pulled me along with him, moving swiftly over the ground toward the distant, rolling downs faintly outlined against the moonlit sky.

"Why didn't you bring my handbag?" I asked, trying to puzzle it out as we rushed through low grass and hard, unyielding ground, away from the inn. "And why can't we go by the road? We could thumb a ride."

He shook his head, and when I could see his face in the moonlight, he explained, "The yellow-haired lady's been at the telephone. Pam and the chap from London was in your room. I knew they'd see your purse when I carried it out, so I emptied it and put the junk in my pockets."

I took *junk* to be another expression he had picked up "on the films," and even in my present circumstances I could not keep from smiling.

"Thanks for the junk, Toddles. And by the way, where are we going?"

"They'll never think of the Stones. Hope you've all your money. I never took it, if you don't have it all."

"I know. Anyway, I shall be quite safe as soon as I can reach the police."

I did not like the way Tod's head moved, as if he disagreed. I was still distributing the contents of Tod's handkerchief between my two coat pockets as we hurried along, and I only half took him seriously. He nudged me and pulled at my coat sleeve. I stared at him, this time giving him all my attention, beginning to suspect I had underestimated the danger—if possible.

"What is it? Won't we be safe in the villages around here?"

"Maybe. But Pam Wattersley's brother is the only

kind of police we have in this part of the country. We ain't too close to the cities, you know. And now—after Pam was goin' over your room, and her friend holdin' hard to the phone and all, I dunno as that Kevin Wattersley's a chap for to lay any trust to."

I pulled my coat collar high up to protect my cheeks against the brisk slap of night wind off the downs, and the gesture made me think of Max. I felt terribly depressed. Without young Tod to give me a vigorous life, I believe I'd have felt desperate. It seemed to me that all I'd done since that awful day in Mr. Putney's shop was either shiver or run. I could not remember a moment when I had felt really secure since I woke up deaf.

Oh, Max—Max . . .

The boy looked at me and then, to my surprise, put out his hand and patted me on the shoulder. When I glanced at him, expecting some new and horrible disclosure, he murmured distinctly, "Don't you cry, mum. I'll get you through it. Old Toddles will."

This really almost broke me up. My new friend was so very dear in his self-confidence. I smiled and thanked him, but my mind reverted to Max, and I went on thinking of him briefly, trying to understand what had happened there.

"He's just driven away and left me to be murdered by those awful—them, I thought. I had done nothing but think up excuses for him since he left me, but out here under the windy sky, it was perfectly clear. He had just driven away and left me. Because if he hadn't, he was lying dead somewhere. There were moments when I almost preferred him to be dead.

Tod helped me around a big hole, camouflaged with grass, and I started to walk up a hill, but the boy caught me and motioned that we walk around the little hump of ground instead. He pointed back to the inn, so I knew, a little late and stupidly, that we would have made a nice silhouette in the moonlight on that rise of ground. The earth underfoot began to be chalky. I wondered if we would leave footprints. However, the boy quite obviously knew what he was doing.

My ankle turned. I picked myself up before falling, and the boy said something critical about my shoes and their heels. I ignored it. It was a little late now for that kind of observation. But his effort to make me understand it had put my mind off Max and onto the immediate danger.

"If we can't count on this Pam What's-Her-Name's brother, we'll call the inspector I know who's often visited me in Richmond. I can leave a message for him." I saw Tod looking at me again and the tension began to rise in me. "Why?" I asked abruptly. "Aren't there any telephones at the Stones' house?"

"The Stones, mum? Ain't a telephone out in the Stones."

"What do you mean, 'out in the Stones'?"

"Them yon. Them's the Stones." He pointed off on the far horizon, toward the ancient Druid stones, or whatever they were, and I found out that we were headed, not for some normal family named Stone who would help us, but up to what looked very like a monstrous prehistoric world, doubtless full of ghosts and other appurtenances of the dead.

Chapter Ten

IF I HADN'T looked back several times, I would have thought we were walking in circles. There seemed to be nothing ahead but a starry sky, now that the moon had risen high, and each gulley below the downs —each vale, I suppose the English called it—looked exactly like the one before. I kept wishing we might walk up over the hills. It would have been much more encouraging to see our goal ahead of us, even if that goal was another glorified graveyard.

I said to Tod once, "What will we do at the Stones?"

"It's a good place to keep to if you don't want a chap to find you. Like the time I broke the lounge window with a . . ."

Whatever he broke the window with, I assumed he said "a cricket bat," but I couldn't be sure. He was too busy assuring me that he had hidden in the Stones for seven hours until the pangs of hunger and his uncle's sharp eyes overcame his fear of a thrashing.

"Yes," I said, "but I must get away to some civilized place for help. I can't keep wandering around old graveyards. The London police, or Scotland Yard, or whoever, will rescue me. I must get hold of Inspector MacLeish."

"Shhh!" Tod put his grubby but not ungentle hand over my mouth.

I stiffened instantly and was silent. He made me follow him, crouching low so that we couldn't be seen over the brow of the hill until we had crossed into a little thicket of bushes and scratchy, stunted trees. There we had a clear view of the row of humpbacked little hills between us and the Druid stones. Tod, still signaling

103

for my silence, pointed toward the hills on the near horizon between us and the Stones.

"It's Uncle and the chap from London."

I put aside some stiff bushes to look out. The two men were striding down toward us, close enough so that I could make out the bushy red hair of Tod's uncle the innkeeper. The other man was the huge blonde fellow who had seemed to be feeble-minded. There was nothing feeble about him now, with his bullish-looking head and face to match. Between them, the two men looked powerful enough to take on a regiment, and certainly more than a match for my friend Toddles and me. At sight of them I ducked backward and almost stepped on Tod. We waited, both of us shaking as the two men approached. They were talking, sometimes together, each man scarcely waiting for the other to finish. Tod's uncle pointed back at the ancient ruins, which they had apparently visited, and the boy nudged me, indicating that they were talking about him; so I supposed that for some reason, the men had business at the Stones. I hoped Toddles and I were not their business.

The two men came nearer and nearer, Tod's uncle taking the big, confident strides of the country man used to the landscape, the other foreign-looking man more careful, looking down, examining the chalky ground before each step. They were so close now that I could have made out the color of their eyes, and Tod and I waited, holding each other's hand, praying a little, I think.

The foreign man paused by the small clump of bushes where we hid. I'm sure Tod was as petrified with fear, as I was. I remember thinking once, *Where is Max? What has happened? Did he really leave me out here to be hideously murdered? Or, more likely, is he already dead?*

The foreign man leaned against the very bushes behind which I was crouching, and while I imagined for a few seconds of tense, breathless waiting that he was about to reach through and fasten those huge fingers into my own flesh, he began to hop on one foot instead. To my intense relief, he unlaced one old-fashioned-looking shoe such as my father wears and hit it hard against the bushes before putting it back on.

Like me, Tod had been holding his breath. Now, he nudged me again and wiped sweat off his freckled nose.

The two men went on talking. They paid no attention to our lifesaving clump of bushes, but when the foreign man had laced up his ankle-high shoe again, he stamped on the ground repeatedly to get his foot properly set in the shoe. This set up a great chalky dust, and to my horror, Tod, crouching close beside me, began to shake. I could see that he did his best to stifle a sneeze. That explosion would really have been the end for us, and his exertions were enormous. He finally managed to pinch his nose and stop the sneeze, but it was a near thing.

Meanwhile, the two men moved away from the bushes, and the boy and I both took deep breaths and silently shook hands. One thing certainly had been proved in all this—I could count upon Tod Humber to the fullest degree.

He shook my arm. "They're gone now. They can't hear us. The wind's against them."

"You were wonderful," I said. "Simply grand. I'm only sorry you're not Irish."

He grinned. "My mother—she was Sligo-born." And we shook hands again.

I looked out after the distant, retreating figures that still loomed, monstrous and evil to me, upon the skyline.

"What were they saying? Did they give any clue?"

He sobered at the recollection. "Uncle Jolyon's one of 'em. They said you'd ruined everything. You'd heard the voice, and if they didn't take care of you before you got well, it'd be too late. How could that be, Miss? I thought you was deaf. How could you've heard their man's voice?"

"It was when I could hear," I explained when he made himself understood in the moonlight. "Did they mention Doctor Brandt? Or anyone else?"

"Just me, about me hiding in the Cave of the Stones. There was some-ut else, too, about how *he'd* have stopped them, and *he* was a fool, and was served proper. Could that be your friend?"

I was terribly afraid it could be. But there was no use agonizing over it without knowing for sure. I said, "Anyway, I want to thank you, Toddles. If I hadn' listened to you, we'd have gone on over the ridge of those hills and run right into those two men."

He was starting to climb up through the vale around and across the distant downs, when I reminded him that our figures might still be seen upon the horizon. But he shook his head, and I followed him, feeling that he had amply demonstrated that he knew what he was doing. When I reached him, I asked if we still were going to the Stones.

"Wouldn't that be dangerous? Where did your uncle and that man come from?"

"There's a track to the village that goes yon, past the bottom of the downs. Likely they'd walk to the village. I can't think what they'd do with goin' to the Stones. Anyway, when we get there, I'll go first. You keep hid."

I looked back as we crossed one of those rolling little hilltops and saw in the far distance the three or four lights of the inn, all blended into one light, like an eye watching us. Something, maybe that look of vast distances, made me feel terribly tired, almost ready to collapse. Almost . . . but not quite. Young Toddles would never have understood such weakness. He was impatient enough over the difficulty I had in hiking with high heels on.

When I turned my ankle yet again, he sighed but generously excused me by the remark that "Females is like that, mostly."

I made what I considered a game effort to reach the

"chalk combe," whatever that was, with a bit of assistance from Toddles, and we soon found ourselves on a hilltop and entering upon an eerie street of stone monuments like little skyscrapers, much taller than the boy or me, and all surrounded by a long, dry ditch, which we had clambered over, not without difficulty. I supposed this must be, on a smaller scale, a place like Stonehenge, but my knowing young friend enlightened me as we moved through strange, gaunt shadows and light toward what goal I couldn't imagine—for I couldn't yet see in any direction the village he had spoken of.

"It isn't like Stonehenge. Not above half, Miss Nona. There's folk here, their bones all cleaned off neat as can be and buried in heaps all along under where we're awalkin'."

I moved more rapidly, forgetting the bit of pain this gave the wrenched muscle in my ankle. It seemed to me in my tired, alarmed, and terribly worried condition that the great shadows hovering over us moved a little, just beyond the periphery of my vision.

"How long ago were they buried?" Then, realizing that he meant in primeval days, I said hurriedly, "I've got to call and get back to London. And I must send the police or someone to find Doctor Brandt."

He stopped long enough to look me up and down. "You'll not make it to the village tonight. You best sleep the rest of the night in the cave, and then we'll make it off to Combe Coster soon as ever the daylight sets in."

"But it should be as soon as possible."

"And maybe meet some of Uncle's friends suddenlike?"

He was right, of course.

We reached the north end of this little street of monuments or whatever the upended, moonlight-shrouded stones might be. The cave was somewhat below the brow of the hill, on the northwesterly side. Its entrance was almost hidden by straggly bushes and a

curious chalk deposit like a fountain and basin that
had gone dry. As we approached, Tod, true to his
warning, became more cautious and put his finger to his
lip. I watched while he went ahead and carefully
stepped across the chalk deposit before pushing aside
the bushes and peering in. Surely, he could see nothing.
It must be pitch-black in there. But he went on looking. When he signaled to me, rather cautiously, to follow him, I did so, stepping down an arrangement of
chalky rocks that served the purpose of stairs. I was
surprised to see that what I had imagined must be a
deep, frightening cave was actually a long, hollowed-
out crescent in the small table of ground upon which
the world of stone had sat since before the rise of re-
corded history. Still, because of its situation on the
side of the rocky table, it was all in shadow, being
especially dark behind the peculiar fountain-and-basin
formation, which, I suspected, had been made by the
dropping of water in ages long past.

"Careful, Miss Nona. It's fair dark at that end of the
cave," Tod warned me.

I said yes, I knew, but at this particular moment I
was concentrating upon a shadow on the top of the
rocky tableland, a shadow that seemed to shift across
the face of what Tod called the cliff. When I was
satisfied that the thing that had aroused my attention
was only the shadow of a monument, one of Tod's
"Stones," I stepped across the chalk fountain and onto
the ledge he called the cave.

It was slippery here, and I seized hold of the sharp,
jagged edge of the rock, felt it break off in my hand
and threw myself forward into the deepest-shadowed
portion of the cave. Here I was able to catch on to the
heavy and fortunately stationary rock, which stopped
me from sliding further.

"Thank heaven!" I murmured, more to myself than
to Tod. "I must sit down. I really must. I'm absolutely
dead."

I went down on my knees and felt around in the

dark for the back wall of the cave, something to lean against, to close my eyes and take a few safe breaths. I had put my hands, palms out, in front of me and felt nothing, but my knees touched something, and I lowered my hands to the rock beneath my body, this time more gingerly, half-expecting to encounter some animal or a coiled snake. My fingers faintly brushed something, a stretch of smooth cloth, like leather, and my hand jumped off almost of its own volition. I gasped, and soon Toddles shook me to attract my attention.

"Don't be scared, Miss. I'm here." I could barely make out his words in the dim light where he stood near the mouth of the cave.

"It isn't that. I touched something, like a man's coat sleeve." I reached over again and found the cloth as Tod crawled to where I was and followed my lead. We made our discovery together, touching the sleeve of a human arm and then the hand, so cold and so stiff that we both had the same idea at the same instant.

"Blimey, Miss! It'll be a dead man!"

"No, no," I told him quickly with far more reassurance than I felt. "Let's drag him out in the moonlight and see if we can do something. He probably fell off that ledge overhead and crawled in here, hurt. Cracked his head, likely enough."

With Tod's help, I got the man out far enough so that we could try to identify him, particularly Tod, since I had no way of guessing that he might be an acquaintance of mine. There was one terrible moment when I wondered if life was so cruel that this could be Max Brandt. But my first sight of the man's hand in the light showed me that my greatest fear had been baseless. I would never have mistaken these long, exceedingly thin, prehensile fingers for the hard, well-shaped hands of Max Brandt that I loved so much.

"Look yon at his face!" exclaimed Tod. "Face like a hand ax."

And then I recognized the man. He had been the

chauffeur of that black Rolls yesterday when they had tried to kidnap me and I had escaped from the car, into the streets of Richmond and the hands of Max Brandt.

"His name is Leecher," I told the boy. "He and a woman tried to kidnap me yesterday. How is he, do you think?"

Tod examined the man in a competent way, though I saw that his hands were as unsteady as mine. "I think he's bought it, Miss Nona. Dead as them bones are over our heads."

I thought of the ancient bones that Tod had so obligingly told me were buried in the ground above us. It seemed to me we were threatened with death on every side and now, even from the heretofore-safe area over our heads.

"What killed him? Can you find a wound?" I asked, speaking as much to myself as to my companion. Together, we turned the man over, and out on the edge of our little cave, his body caught the light from the open sky. Aside from superficial scratches and bruises on the man's knuckles, face, and wherever his flesh has been bare and might have touched the sharp rocks, we found only one wound that seemed serious enough to have caused his death. It was a singularly unpleasant place on the back of his head, somewhat above the nape of his neck.

"Somebody bashed in his skull is what it was," Tod remarked in a matter-of-fact voice that showed a technical interest in such bloodcurdling details.

I reminded him, "It could have been made when he fell," but I didn't really believe it. I knew perfectly well that Tod's Uncle Jolyon and the big foreign-looking man had enticed their victim out here on one pretext or another and then, to borrow Tod's picturesque phrase, "bashed his skull in."

And for what purpose? I was their enemy. And Max was. At least, he had rescued me from them. But Leecher, this ax-faced man, as Tod called him, was one of them. He had helped that infamous Nurse Tusingham, the worst, the most monstrous of my enemies, and yet these others, surely members of the same group, had killed him.

"I guess it was a case of the falling out of thieves," I explained to Tod, who didn't understand the significance. He had a child's morbid curiosity about the wound itself and kept examining it and making boyishly gruesome comments. I did not stop him. My own mind was full of the confusions I had experienced, not only since the day of my deafness but just since yesterday. Nothing fitted. It was all a senseless jumble, all but the danger.

Suddenly, Tod seemed to realize the implication closest to his own life, and his fingers stopped their quick, eager, curious movements. He raised his eyes to me. This time he looked so troubled that I felt all his misery and longed to comfort him, though there was little I could do. Poor Tod! Morally, his problem was worse than mine.

He said, "Uncle's in it."

"I know, Toddles."

"Uncle's done things before, but not . . . like this. He's a murderer. They'll put him to prison forever. I seen how it is around the prison on Dartmoor. Fair gives you the shivers."

I put out my hand to his briefly, feeling the uselessness of my sympathy. He began to make excuses, the next step before the final conviction in his own mind.

" 'Course, maybe he'd nothing to do with it. The axfaced man could've fallen. Easy."

"No, Tod. We must be honest between ourselves. We both saw those two men returning from the Stones. They must have known about Leecher. Leecher was one of *them.*"

"Maybe Uncle and the other man were comin' from Combe Coster. Uncle goes to the village every day."

"And every night?"

He was honest enough not to go into any more excuses. We went over the body as much as we could, both of us hoping, mostly for the sake of Tod's uncle, that this Leecher, somehow, was not really dead yet. He was, though. Tod was right. I'd never seen a dead man in my life except that cat burglar whom Max Brandt had killed in my room on Richmond Hill, but the cold, the rigidity, the general look of Leecher's flesh made the thing certain.

"What'll we do, Miss, leave him here?" asked Tod hopefully. "Maybe we could just make as if we'd not seen 'im. Then, when he's found, nobody'd know about Uncle being—"

"Never mind that. We've simply got to get to that village you spoke of."

"Combe Coster? But it's so far in the dark. You'd never make it, Miss. You're that tired! And, anyway, I can't be doin' a thing that'll put Uncle to prison."

I was more aware of our long and strenuous walk than he was.

"We've got to. We're safer there, with normal citizens, than out here with no witnesses. Don't you see, Tod, any of them could kill us there, at any minute, and no one to help us. No one even to hear us."

He was obviously still brooding over his betrayal of his murderous uncle, because he poured out a great deal of protest and objection, which I neither heard nor understood.

"Toddles, this isn't the films, as you call it. Those people are working to betray your own country."

"Not Uncle. He was in the war. I mean—they must be making him do it. Well . . ." He knew we had to do as I said.

We moved Leecher's body back into the darkness, and though both of us were aching with the strain and the fright of these past hours, we managed to make our way out and up those improvised chalky steps. Tod scrambled up first, and I followed as before, but a little more tired, a little more shaken than before. Tod stood above me, grabbing hold of one of those skyscraper blocks of stone and swinging from it to offer me a hand up.

I took the hand he offered and drew myself up once more into that strange world of stone, shadow, and moonlight. Tod had his back to the Stones and therefore didn't notice, as I noticed now, with a chilling slowness, that we were being watched and had been watched, probably since I had first seen that moving shadow when we climbed down to the cave.

Chapter Eleven

My FIRST and obvious thought was for a weapon. It would be very easy for that figure in the deep shadow of the stone monument to lean forward and give a single heavy shove, sending Tod over the cliff and me with him. Without betraying my awareness of the watcher, I reached into my two pockets. There seemed to be nothing. My fingers fastened around the only possible weapon, my powder compact made from a snuff box, in which I carried loose powder, having recently switched over from my usual pressed powder. I was grateful for that switch now.

Tod reached out for me again.

"Miss Nona, come along. It's ever so far. We best be off or the moon'll go down."

I tried to make some inane comment that would satisfy him while I was bracing myself for the all-important moment to come.

"Thank you, Tod." I got safely on the tableland so that whoever was watching us would have to make two moves. He could not get us both at once. He was beginning to move out of the lengthening shadows now, and I saw that he was at this minute more dangerous to me than anyone else in the gang of traitors—for it was Tod's Uncle Jolyon, his red hair bristling in the windy night. His huge, muscular arm, revealed by his rolled-up shirt sleeves, looked more imposing, more frightening than ever, as he took a step closer to us. I kept my hands in my pockets, ready.

Tod, seeing my stare, looked around, saw his Uncle and cried out eagerly, "Oh, Uncle Jolyon! I knew you wasn't in it with them! We're ever so glad to see you.

We're in awful trouble. They want to kill Miss Nona."
To me, Tod explained ingenuously, "You see, mum, if
Uncle was like you thought he was, he wouldn't come
back to fetch us, would you, sir?"

How the boy could think that when he saw the big
man's eyes glistening at us like that, I lay only to his
family devotion.

"Toddles, you are to go home to the inn. Get off
now!" The man made as if to swat Tod, who looked
from him to me, smiling uncertainly. "But Uncle—
what about Miss Nona? I'd as soon—"

"Get off, boy!"

Then, as Tod took a step or two and turned back
for one last effort, and I knew I had lost him to his
natural trust in his family, the man said roughly, "I'm
to see Miss off as far as Combe Coster. It's what's
wanted by her doctor friend."

"Aye. That'll do fine, sir. You see, Miss Nona? Uncle's on our side. Uncle, did you know there's a dead
man below in my cave?"

I groaned silently but hoped I did not show my fury
and fright at this disclosure. I thought I had to give
the man the benefit of my last doubt.

Before I could speak, however, he said brusquely,
in answer to his nephew, "I knew. A visitor I took
hunting discovered the body. He has gone for help.
Pam said she saw you start out here with the doctor's
patient. I came back. Toddles, you know you're not to
be out here at night."

"Sir," I put in, trying not to let my quick inter-
ruption sound like fear, "please let your nephew go
with us to Combe Coster." This, at least, would help
to prove the man was sincere, which I very much
doubted.

"Off!" said the man to Tod, who jumped guiltily
and obeyed him, scuffing along in the direction from
which we had come, while the man himself reached
out one huge hand to me as if, politely, to help me
along. I assumed that in one thing he told the truth.

He was alone. Otherwise, the tough, blond foreign man would be handling me and the innkeeper would simply return home with his gullible nephew.

While I stalled for time, knowing I would have to be out of reach of him when I started to run, I asked innocently, "Did Doctor Brandt say why he drove to Combe Coster? I've looked everywhere for him."

Behind him, Tod Humber was already scuttling off the opposite end of the Stones into the darkness, beyond the point where he could still hear us. I could see that he was used to the overwhelming personality of his uncle and had seldom disobeyed him. I had very little time left.

Uncle Jolyon grinned in that toothy way which promised all kinds of unpleasantness. I could imagine how much he and his gang hated me after all the difficulties I had made for them by refusing to die.

"Come now, Miss. You're a big lass. You know what's expected. You gave us a bit of a chase."

"I—I don't understand," I lied. "Why did Max leave the inn alone? He would never have gone without me."

"Give us your hand. There's a good lass. It'll all be over, quick as a wink. . . . And very like, you'll be meeting your precious Max."

I pretended to misunderstand, and reached for his hairy fingers with my left hand, my right being still in my pocket. He leaned forward, since I had carefully missed touching him, and in that fraction of time, when he was off-balance, I pulled my right hand out of my pocket, with the snuff box open, and threw the full case of powder hard upward, into those glistening eyes of his. He tottered, thrown further off his balance by the shock of the powder, which ground into his wide-open eyes, making him cough and grope blindly for me. I was sure he made horrible noises, yelling and cursing, but since I could not hear them and was off on the run immediately, I've no idea how long this maddened dance of his continued.

I knew that as soon as he could see again, which

would only be a matter of a few minutes at the longest, he would be after me and on the path over the downs, to Combe Coster. On the other hand, I could hardly return to that inn with its deadly company. I rushed into the darkness of a distant stone monument and looked over the edge. Here it was all rolling slopes and easy to descend. My impetus carried me a long way down the slope and into the enormous dark of the heath. I knew I was headed in the general direction where Toddles had pointed out the path to the village of Combe Coster. I began to make out the path itself, dimly, no more than a sheep track and winding along in a general westerly direction. I followed it on lower ground between the rolling hills, remembering Tod's hint that it was easier to be seen on high ground.

I had run a very long distance, it seemed to me, before my legs gave out, and finding a sheltered little hollow with a view of the Combe Coster path above me, I slumped down upon the hard, unyielding heath and felt an enormous throbbing ache clear through my body.

I'll rest just a few minutes, I thought. *I must be off this desolate heath before dawn.* It would be easy enough to avoid being seen in this starry night, with the moon already going down, but once it was daylight I could be seen for miles.

I closed my eyes momentarily, grateful for the velvety oblivion I felt at once.

I remember dreaming. I was in a very cold place, far in the north, and running and running, exhausted, crying out to Dr. Max Brandt, who stood in the far distance, impassively watching me and making no effort to help me. The weather in my dream was so frightful that I found myself shaking, and this shaking brought me back to consciousness, stiff as a board and very nearly frozen into one.

It was a little after dawn. A very familiar-looking uniform knelt over me, rather like that of a London bobby, with an odd helmet and chinstrap to top off the comfortably safe look. The chubby face outlined by the chinstrap, however, was not familiar.

"Who are you?" I asked and I hoped I spoke aloud.

"I'm constable in these parts, Miss. You'll be the lady Doctor Brandt has set me on to find. The lady what can't hear?"

"Doctor Brandt?" I asked excitedly, feeling a restoration of body and spirit. "You know he is all right?"

"Right as a trivet, mum. Said he'd gone off to Combe Coster on an errand like, and when he come back, you'd been and run off. Can you stand? There's a girl."

"Where is he now?"

"He's up and down Combe Coster road in his little runabout. We agreed I was to take the Stones path and he'd take the road. You'd have to go one way or other."

How plausible it all was! Only one thing I couldn't understand—what errand had been so pressing that it took Max away from the inn just when he and I were in such great danger?

No matter. The constable's chubby, good-humored face and rotund shape were very reassuring.

"Hard put to get on your feet, Miss? That'll be the night damp and the tiredness." He spoke very clearly, framing every syllable so that I could not doubt that Max, or *someone,* had told him of my hearing difficulty. Apparently, if it had been Max, the doctor had not told him of our danger, because he made no mention of arresting anyone at the inn or, indeed, of anything criminal in the whole district. He must surely have wondered why I ran away over this endless heath. At any rate, I appreciated his kindness and his help. I got up. The constable brushed me off, and I was stiff all over, along with a soreness in one ankle that made the long walk ahead seem a nightmare. Still, if I was to meet Max at the end of that walk, and find he had a reasonable excuse for his inexcusable desertion, I felt I could walk halfway across England.

I was so confused when I started out that after a

few steps, I suddenly found myself limping eastward toward the distant Stones, and I stopped abruptly.

"Constable—I'm sorry, I don't know your name. . . . Why didn't you stop me? I was headed the wrong way."

"Really, Miss? Oh, I shouldn't think too much on that. You see, it might be the best thing for you, back to the inn. Pam says you've been fair sick and were a bit more at home in your room at the inn. I could drive Pam's car back to fetch your doctor.

I shivered and turned around, facing what I supposed must be the village of Combe Coster.

"If there is any place out here that has telephones . . ."

"Telephones, Miss, out here?" His curly eyebrows went up and I had to explain hurriedly.

"It's because of that man's body. It should be got down immediately, if only Humber and his friends don't do away with it first—"

"Body, Miss?"

"Yes. His name is Leecher. A man from London who tried to kidnap me."

The constable seemed unconcerned. "Yes, yes. That body. All snug, Miss. What's the thing to do now is get you back to someplace where you'll be able to rest. Doctor says you've been hard put."

"But Leecher's body!" I protested, and then thought I understood. "Did someone report the man's death? Tod Humber was with me when we discovered it. Tod must have—"

" 'Twas he that told me. Just so. Just so." He nodded emphatically and tried to help me along. "If you're still feeling a bit rough, Miss, then we'd best get to the inn."

"I couldn't possibly go back to the inn, and I'm not going to allow you to take me either. I will scream and kick and yell and . . ." Almost too belatedly, I understood a fact that had been tucked away in his explanation to me. "What name did you mention a minute ago —Pam?"

"Me, Miss? That'll be my sister. Wattersley's the name. Constable Wattersley. Now, if you're not for the inn, we'll go on as planned, over the downs to Combe Coster. Let's give you a little lift-over, as you might say."

There was no point in his going on to explain his relationship to that deadly sister of his, Pam Wattersley. If he intended to kill me as Pam and the rest of *"them"* had killed Leecher—for what reason I couldn't imagine —he could must more easily have murdered me while I slept. But he hadn't.

Poor Constable Wattersley tried to cheer me up on that hike over what I persistently referred to in my mind as the "darkling heath," by talking a great deal. But he was always forgetting that I couldn't hear him, nor could I read his lips when he was facing the same direction that I was; so I just put one tired, aching foot before the other and made no reply.

A thick, low fog gathered over the downs in great puffs and seemed to cling to my face and hands and my legs. By the time the constable was able to point out the distant thatched roofs that marked Combe Coster, I felt that I had crossed an entire English county. At sight of those rooftops, I began to pull my tired wits together, trying to decide how I could report with safety the death of Leecher and my own proofs, whatever they might be, against the residents of the inn. Whether poor Tod Humber would back me up about the things we had seen, I did not know. Already, his uncle had talked him out of any suspicions in that quarter.

My only real hope was Max, of course, as always. He would know what we should do about my own attempted murder. The really incredible thing was that with all the crimes that had occurred to me and around me, I hadn't one solid piece of evidence to prove any of that murderous crowd guilty.

"First, after I meet Max," I said as we entered the

quaint, picturesque little town, "I must make a trunk call to London."

"Well, Miss, that'll be at the stationer's. Miss Nettings, that is."

Not a stationer! I thought. That was how it had all started, with Mr. Putney and his shop. But I was too grateful to make objections on the mere ground of my sensitivity, grateful to the constable and to this little village with its single curving street, its white cottages side by side like Papa's Irish coteens, and to the people here—thank heaven for these people! They looked so normal, so little like the sinister and silent face of death with which I had been daily, even hourly surrounded! Now, where was Max?

At my question, the constable looked around the local pub, which was empty at this early hour, and I suggested that we look for Max's little deep red MG. One of the constable's street acquaintances, a middle-aged, black-clad shopkeeper opening his greengrocer's shop, gave us the information we were beginning to suspect.

"The gent with the fancy little London runabout? Aye. He was that strung up, on the look for a lady, he said. He took his runabout and buzzed off to that pub where your sister works, Wattersley."

"You see? Just as I said," the constable reminded me.

"Then I must make my phone call. I really can't wait," I said nervously. "And I will need help with their reply. Constable, could you possibly stay until I've made the call, so that if I am in the stationer's when Doctor Brandt comes, you can tell him?"

Constable Wattersley said his duties took him out of doors in any case, and he would be glad to oblige me. Meanwhile, he felt sure my telephone call could be handled by little Miss Nettings, the lady who owned the stationer's shop. I went in and we were made acquainted. The lady, a tiny, shriveled, pert woman of sixty or so, assured me that she would be happy to oblige in any way.

I set out enough pound notes I found wadded carelessly in my pockets, and placed them beside the telephone. The call required three different connections,
until we finally got someone who reported, according
to Miss Nettings, that Inspector MacLeish was out but
that the call would be reported to him and the voice on
the other end of the line would be happy to convey any
information I cared to leave. Miss Nettings became extremely excited over this, looking at me with new admiration. Obviously, she was impressed at any connection, however vague, with Scotland Yard.

There was nothing for it but to wait for Max and
to hope Constable Wattersley was not merely humoring
me when he spoke of having located and taken care of
Leecher's body. Hoping to learn a little more about
the reputation of that nice and obliging little Constable
Wattersley, I asked Miss Nettings, "Has the constable
held his job very long?"

"Oh, my, yes. Since time out of mind. A lovely
man."

I would hardly have called the roly-poly little man
"lovely," but I assumed this was a compliment of no
mean degree.

"And his sister, that girl at the inn across the
moors?"

"My dear! Not the moors. The downs. But to answer your question, Pamela is . . . well . . ." She lowered her head and I suspected lowered her voice at the
same time. At any rate, I understood what she meant
as she enunciated with great precision, snapping her
false teeth, "Pam is one of *those* girls! Always was.
Now she's corrupted—the very word, my dear—corrupted that rough character, Jolyon Humber."

I agreed promptly, adding that it was a disease that
spread, because Jolyon Humber had corrupted his
nephew to a state where Tod Humber believed him even
over the evidence of a dead body and his uncle's very
suspicious presence.

"Did the constable bring in a dead body from the downs last night? Have you heard rumors? Anything?"

Miss Nettings's eyes grew round in their wrinkled frame. She leaned closer to me and whispered all sorts of details about Pam Wattersley's peccadilloes, none of which I understood, but she did remind me of one thing. Constable Wattersley's abrupt dismissal of my report on the dead Leecher, along with the obvious fact that the body had not been reported, suggested that he thought I was sick and imagining the whole business of the dead man.

Something had to be done at once, officially, and I was very much afraid Constable Wattersley was not the man for it. I had failed to get Scotty at his London headquarters, but there was one more chance. He had been very often at Richmond, and even if he was not, he might keep in contact with it, knowing that I had disappeared from there.

"Miss Nettings, will you place another call for me, this time to Richmond? It's quite literally a matter of life and death."

"Of course. You've only to ask. I should be most happy. It's quite like the war days."

I gave her the hotel name, and she called and, at my direction, asked for Detective Inspector MacLeish. I was far from surprised to learn from Miss Nettings that he was not there, but then, there was a little pause, an apparent discussion on the other end of the phone.

"Leave a message," I put in quickly. "Ask the operator to have Inspector MacLeish call me here as soon as possible."

Little Miss Nettings stood on tiptoes to repeat my instructions. She paused now and looked at me. "Shall I give this number?"

"Please do. When Doctor Brandt comes, I'll see to it that one of us is here. I want to report a murder to the police. They will contact someone in this area."

So Miss Nettings, showing every sign of pride in her unusual work, consulted her own book of telephone numbers and, being assured of the facts, repeated her own number.

I asked nervously, "Inspector MacLeish wasn't at the hotel in Richmond?"

"No, dear. But he is expected. They said he has been at the hotel you named four times since two days ago." She was dying of curiosity. I could see that.

Someone knocked on the window. We both looked out. Constable Wattersley came around and, finding the door ajar, called to us, "That red runabout your doctor was driving—it's on the way, Miss O'Carty. Saw it up the road."

"There," Miss Nettings assured me. "You see, it is all safe and sound now. And soon your Inspector Mac-Leish will receive your message and solve it all."

I ran to the door, hardly believing in my luck. I was to see Max Brandt again. He had not died, or deserted me, or been murdered. Together, we would see to it that all of *"them"* were captured and that there was safety for us again, after the nightmare days.

I reached the door, then turned back briefly to reassure myself on the exceedingly important matter of Scott's being informed.

"You did tell the hotel operator where I was, precisely, didn't you? The inspector should be here late today."

"I told her exactly what you said, dear. She was most grateful."

I started out the door, but she had not finished speaking. I looked back and watched her nervously, with an effort to remain patient.

"It was even better than the hotel operator," she said. "It was a lady from Inspector MacLeish's office who was there when we called. I talked to her."

"Good. Who was it?"

"She asked particularly where you were now. I was happy to tell her. It was a nurse named Bertha Tusingham."

Chapter Twelve

"Nот—!" I could hardly get it out. "Miss Nettings, you didn't say Nurse Tusingham!"

"That very name. Don't tell me you know the lady! What a happy coincidence! Ah, but please look behind you, Miss O'Carty. There he is! No sooner mention his name than he appears like magic."

I had a dreadful expectation of seeing Nurse Bertha Tusingham standing there on the street behind me, her blue cape flying like a bat's wings. But before I could limp out to the street to face her, I felt a hand upon my shoulder and just barely stifled a scream as I turned.

Max Brandt bent his head and kissed me twice, first on my lips, which must have felt cooled by the foggy weather, and then on the knuckles of my shivering hand. I was overwhelmed as much by his presence and his vitality as by the unusual gentleness of his gesture, and I returned his embrace with all the passion in my starved and heretofore frightened senses, my hands no longer trembling, my lips far from cold.

But when we drew apart a trifle, with his arm still around my waist and me feeling protected and safe for the first time in what seemed an eternity, he was abrupt, almost angry as we left the shop.

"Nona, why did you leave? Do you know what I went through during these past hours? I've been over that road, gone through that inn with this Wattersley fellow from cellar to attic . . . half-expecting to find your body!"

"Don't say it! It nearly happened. Where did you go? I waited and waited."

His hard, sardonic features softened in that special

way I had noticed occasionally when he looked at me.
I was sickeningly conscious now that this gentleness,
so unlike the normal look and manner of Max Brandt,
was directed at the image of the dead Ilona that he
saw in me. But feeling for him as I did, I was moved by
this as I was by any sign of his genuine affection for
me. At that moment of my intense relief, I chose to believe that this wonderful and very special look in his
usually hard eyes was entirely for me.

"Come along, *Liebchen*. We must find you a breakfast of sorts, and we'll plan our next move." He seemed
to say this rather loudly—at least, I had the feeling that
his words, which I guessed at, were said for the benefit
of passersby.

"It was horrible," I told him as we walked. I did not
mind his long strides or his hurry, for he was always
thoughtful enough to help me and take most of the
pressure off my tired, twisted ankle. Nevertheless, I
could not help wondering at his extreme haste.

We passed one cozy little café that seemed to spe-
cialize uncharacteristically, in coffee, whose wonderful
fresh aroma I could smell clear out in the street. We
did not stop in there, however. We went on to a little
path that led to a small inn or pub on the outskirts of
the village. Around us on every side, I saw in the distance the sloping downs, the enormous stretches of
space so sparsely settled that I would have called them
moors. Everything I saw reminded me of last night,
those great monoliths of prehistoric man, and above
all, the dead body of Leecher.

"What is to be done about the body Tod and I
found?" I asked when I saw he was headed toward that
outlying little pub with its gloomy atmosphere of loneliness and unpopularity among the villagers.

"Wattersley mentioned Leecher. Don't concern
yourself with it," Max told me in his brusque, comforting positive way. "That funny little constable will
take care of the matter. He told me so."

"Yes, but he didn't believe me. I'm sure of it. Only

Tod, that boy, and I saw the man dead. And when I mentioned it to the constable, he seemed very odd. He simply dismissed it."

Max was looking around, down the road, and suddenly I realized that he had no interest in this out-of-the-way pub. He was heading for his red MG, which he had parked along a pebble-strewn, chalky shoulder of the smoothed-out parking place behind the pub, in a spot that couldn't be seen from the highway. I looked around, bewildered. We had already passed beyond the confines of the village and were encompassed by the dreary, monotonous, rolling landscape, green now in spring but almost as unnerving as the Stones that Tod and I had fled to last night.

"Are we going to have breakfast here? I wish we needn't."

He looked at me. Curiosity was blended with a kind of intense quality that troubled me. "Aren't you hungry? You look as though you could use a good cup of tea, at least."

I thought nothing would have looked or smelled better than that coffee whose aroma we had passed by so quickly. But I did not like to say so, since, for some reason, he had preferred to pass by the place in the village. Perhaps he thought this isolated house would be safer. But in that case, he hadn't taken into consideration the presence of decent villagers plus, above all, the constable himself.

When I didn't say anything to Max's suggestion, he glanced over at the MG and then said suddenly, "I want to get you away before the rest of them arrive. Anything can happen, with all of them involved!"

"But the constable!"

He smiled, that now-familiar smile which showed very little humor. The collar of his dark coat, pulled high around his face, made him look more somber, even sinister, than I remembered.

"He is hardly a match for all of them. Besides, there is sure to be unpleasantness about the fellow who was killed. We'll have something hot to drink, then be on the way and stop for breakfast as soon as it looks safe."

I began to feel that he hadn't told me everything he knew about Leecher's death, and I was still waiting for his explanation about last night's desertion. "Why did you leave me last evening? You said you would tell me."

He did not reply until we were passing his car, and I had to look into his face to understand him. "I'm sorry. I saw one of the men . . . that fellow Leecher that you disliked, and started after him. I'm afraid I lost him at some point on the road between the inn and Combe Coster."

I could hardly believe this.

"How horrible! He must have been murdered between the time you lost him and several hours later when Tod and I saw him on that place they call the Stones."

He did not look at me, so I could not tell what he said in answer. In fact, now that I thought of it, he had not really looked at me since we left the foggy gray of the village. But it might be that he merely wanted to get me away in a hurry. As for me, I still wanted to wait in the village, where we were surrounded by help. Then I remembered the telephone calls to London.

"I'm sure we are expected to stay here, Max. You see, I called Scotty in London. And he's sure to——"

This time he did look at me. I thought for a minute he was going to shake me. "Are you completely mad?"

Confused and angered at his unmistakable reaction, I said sharply, "No! I found a dead man and I reported it. That stupid constable did nothing. I've been pursued and threatened and I don't know what all. Anyway, I didn't get Scotty."

He seemed to have recovered by this time and explained something about local people hearing me on the phone and betraying my position to *them*. But I was no longer interested in his bursts of temper, and

I did not believe that sweet, wizened little Miss Nettings was out to eavesdrop on me and report me to *them*.

In Max's excitement, he had turned to me quickly; the black collar of his coat twisted and folded back, and I saw a long black-and-blue bruise at the side of his head, from his hairline to his jaw.

"Max! What happened? Were you hurt?"

Impatiently, he turned up his collar. "No, no. It was last night. A near collision on the road."

"After you left me." I said it flatly, suspiciously. I didn't know why it upset me, beyond the obvious worry over his safety and health, but I felt that there was a great deal he had not told me.

"So you didn't reach Scotty," he observed, leading me into the pub through a rear door. The house was old and musty but smelled deliciously of frying bacon and eggs and browning toast. "We'll contact the police when we reach the coast."

"The coast! Where are we going?"

"Ireland. It's all we can reach in safety, without your being held on that other business."

"You mean by being a witness? The business about Mr. Putney?"

"No! I mean——" He stopped and appeared to change his tack. "Yes. About the Putney business. Come along."

I thought what we were doing was terribly dangerous, trying to outwit the police as well as that pack of traitors, and besides, I was sure Max hadn't been about to mention the Putney case. But I went along with him, making no further objections. Perhaps, after all, he would save me, and then I would know him well enough to feel I could marry him. Even I recognized now that my first infatuation had not been quite enough for a lifetime together. There were other qualities in him that I loved, and when, as now, I found myself loving and excusing his temper and his abruptness, I felt that I had not been too hasty, after all, when I thought after such short acquaintance that I could be happy with him all my life.

We did eat breakfast, after all. I think the wonderful aroma was too much for even the determined Max. We ate in the kitchen of the funny little pub, and Max topped his breakfast off with beer, of all things, while I ate. It was done very rapidly. He was in great haste. Then, when we got into his little car and started off, I noticed that we soon turned off on a bumpy, ill-defined road that seemed to me little better than the horrible path Tod and I had taken last night. At last, though, I was with Max Brandt now, and he wouldn't desert me as the boy had.

He drove at such speed that you would have thought he was timing himself. Very soon, while it was still morning, we were at the border of the county. It had been impossible for him to make any explanations, as it was impossible for me to hear or understand them. We both gave big sighs when we saw a neat little inn with the new county's name on it, and then, just as I was making some remark about my relief, Max looked in the rear-view mirror and, to my dismay, suddenly braked the car and slapped the wheel angrily.

We stopped in the center of the little road because behind us, a larger, older car was signaling, and I recognized the man beside the driver. He was Constable Wattersley, and he got out and came toward us much faster than I would have thought possible to anyone so plump.

I looked at Max, feeling the helpless panic of not hearing what was said when he and Constable Wattersley talked back and forth, the constable looking in over the car door and saying something severe but polite to Max.

"What is it?" I asked nervously. "Have they caught us speeding or something?"

Max said to me with his wonderful, confident manner, "It is all ridiculous. A trick by Jolyon Humber, backed by that ward of his."

"You mean, it is about the body we found? That Leecher?"

"They have questions."

"But Tod saw it too. He was with me."

Max spoke to the constable, who kept talking back and pointing to me. I knew perfectly well he was telling me my duty, reminding me that I had committed an offense of some sort. I knew, even before he began, that we were going to have to return to that place where I had experienced such horror.

Max looked like thunder and didn't seem inclined to explain the trouble to me, so I leaned over and studied the constable, whose innocent face looked as if it were stained with a continuous blush.

"Have you heard from London about my calls? I tried to contact Detective Inspector MacLeish."

"Yes, Miss. That's the way of it. That and the business what's got to be cleared up, as you might say, about the alleged body of the alleged Eston Leecher."

"What do you mean alleged? Tod Humber and I both saw it. There can be no doubt about the body. How it was killed is another matter."

"One thing's sure and certain, Miss. The chap's not reported back to his landlady, and there's a stir getting up about him."

"I should think there would be!" I began and would have gone on, except for Max's interference.

"Nona! Don't discuss the Leecher business. Do you understand me? Don't discuss it in any way. All right, Constable. We'll return to Combe Coster, but I assure you that if anything happens, anything at all, to Miss O'Carty, I will hold you responsible. She is in grave danger because of something that she witnessed near London."

He went on a bit, but it was a strain for me to follow this torrent of angry protests, and I gave up. Shortly afterward, Max turned the car around and we drove back toward Combe Coster through the lonely countryside, while cold fingers of panic seemed to squeeze my

heart again, and I wondered if I would ever escape entirely from the long reach of that conspirators' group.

Max liked it even less than I did when Constable
Wattersley got into the other car and saw to it that we
did not turn off at any side roads or otherwise try
to "escape his custody," as I thought of it. On that
nerve-racking trip Max put out his hand, found mine on
the car seat, and squeezed it. Then he slapped it lightly,
and looking at me, he said, "I don't know what they
have in mind for us, but we must be prepared, darling."

To hear him call me "darling" with that special light
in his eyes was worth all the danger we faced. I smiled,
said confidently, "I understand. I'm prepared," and sat
up straighter, planning just how bravely I would behave, to be worthy not only of my parents, who had
faced their own enormous dangers at my age, but of
Max Brandt, as well. He probably thought me a coward
and always in difficulties. He would soon see, I promised myself.

The village, although busier, appeared just as calm
as it had been when we left it. I saw the greengrocer
sweeping out his shop, and Miss Nettings was talking
enthusiastically to a stout, tweedy female customer. Yet
in spite of the calm, there was over the village and the
quaint houses, even over the people, a kind of brown
mist. I took it to be the fog, combined with a wind that
blew off the chalk downs and formed a smoggy atmosphere, but I had never known such an oppressive
feeling, and I wondered if Max too was influenced by
it.

"Why won't anyone believe me about *them?*" I asked
Max as we entered town. "They should all be behind
bars or something."

"They will be 'or something,' I promise you," Max
told me grimly, which only made me laugh, though I
suspected he hadn't intended his remark that way. At
any rate, I was grateful for this brief interlude before
what I was beginning to look upon as my final con-
frontation with those murderers. By his confidence and

certainty, Max almost, but not quite, destroyed that strange, misty pall of brown death which I saw everywhere as we drove into the village—a pall I felt was directed in some uncanny way at me.

Max parked the car on the street beyond a small two-story hotel, and we came around by a chalk path to the main street of the village, where I became aware that I was the object of some eerie concern on the part of those same people who had, an hour ago, been gracious and friendly. Now, as I walked into their view, they gathered in little groups and talked about me so plainly that I felt sure Max heard them. He went to rather obvious precautions over keeping me away from them, even standing between me and the villagers, forgetting, I suppose, that I could not hear their comments.

Wattersley came to join us immediately. He looked embarrassed, as he should be. "Shall we all take seat in the lounge of the Coster Hotel? There'll be a few matters that need settling. You know how it is."

"No. I don't," said Max, so succinctly that I could almost hear the words. "If Miss O'Carty is not protected, you will be held strictly accountable. . . . You know how *that* is."

"Certainly, certainly. No harm will come to Miss O'Carty. Quite the other way about, but more of that later. Come along in."

There was mystery in that remark, but I did not pursue it. Besides, it was possible I had misunderstood him.

The greengrocer, in his forbidding black, moved away from his shop and said something to Miss Nettings and her customer, and they all looked at me. It was so obvious that I took hold of Max's coat sleeve. He covered my hand with his. He was furious. I could see that by his tension and by the frightening look of his mouth, set and contemptuous. He glanced through the brown swirls of fog at the townspeople, one group at a time. There was a buzzing conversation among them that, when combine with Max's extraordinary hatred, made me sure they were discussing me in no pleasant way.

Max ushered me up the steps and into the gloomy little hall, which smelled strongly of boiling cabbage.

"What is it?" I whispered uneasily. "If it's about me, I wish you'd tell me."

He motioned me to silence just as I saw that the front parlor seemed to be full of people. The true significance didn't quite penetrate my confused brain for a few seconds. The pretty, curvacious brunet of the Humber Inn was there, buried in a worn, overstuffed rocking chair. Behind the chair was Jolyon Humber, his red hair standing on end, his big teeth flashing even when, as now, he did not smile. There was a hard blond woman I couldn't place, and the square-faced foreign man whom Tod and I had seen last night returning from the murdered man on the Stones.

"But—but . . . they're all the people who want to kill me," I stammered as Constable Wattersley made a polite gesture, asking us to join that bloodcurdling group.

The constable looked at me directly. I could not mistake his words. "Miss, are we to believe that each and all of these good people want to kill you? Why, one of them is my own sister, my own little Pam!"

My knees felt shaky. Max guessed it and gave my hand a hard, firm pressure, lending me courage. I shrugged and walked into the parlor with him.

Chapter Thirteen

By THE TIME we were in that parlor, encircled by creatures I regarded with revulsion, to say the least, I had borrowed some of Max's deep anger. I pointed stiffly at Jolyon Humber and then at the foreign blond man.

"Ask these two about that dead man out on the Stones. They were returning from there when Mr. Humber's nephew and I saw them."

I wondered if I could count upon Tod. He was missing now, and he had let me down last night.

The constable said something in a pacifying way, first to me and then to the two I accused. I ignored him as I ignored the chair Jolyon Humber offered me with an ostentatious gesture of chivalry. The big, toothy smile that accompanied his gesture, however, promised me certain unpleasantnesses on some happy occasion when we were alone. I did not intend to let him get me alone.

Max pulled another chair out for me, and I sat down. Then Max spoke to Constable Wattersley. I did not see what he said at first, but then I picked up the thread of it.

"Constable, why did you call Miss O'Carty back here? And what have these people to do with it?"

I cut in, "Don't be so polite, Max. You know perfectly well these people are part of that gang in Richmond that tried to kill me. They are still trying."

The brunet girl, Pam Wattersley, said something, and Constable Wattersley waved a pudgy hand.

"Right you are, Pam. To the point. Very true. This is how it is, Doctor Brandt—there's been a deal of talk about this man Leecher. I've been out to the Stones with Humber. There's nothing there. He took one side and I took the other. We found nothing."

Of course you found nothing! I thought. *The criminal himself was helping you to find nothing!*

The constable very obviously did not read my thoughts. He went on, feeling very official, I've no doubt, "All the same, this Leecher does exist, and he is missing. There's no denying that. And it's my duty to see that Miss O'Carty stays in the country until we find the chap."

"But what have I to do with it, unless—" Belatedly, I thought I knew. "Because I am a witness, of course. But Tod, the boy, was a witness. Couldn't he . . . ?"

"Not as a witness, I'm afraid, Miss. Your presence here is . . . as a principal, so to speak."

I sat up with a stiff-backed poise. Max put a hand on the nape of my neck, gently, firmly, but for once I paid no attention to his restraining touch.

"I don't understand. What do you mean by that?"

"Well, Miss, we've a bit of a problem. You see, no one else here knows this Leecher, except you. You are the only tie Leecher has to Combe Coster. Pam tells me you knew Leecher in London and hated him. Then he followed you here. . . . Now he's disappeared, and you tell me he's dead. What am I to think?"

I looked at the brunet girl. She returned my attention with an insolent half smile.

I said to the constable, while looking at his sister, "You may think what you please. And who, by the way, mentioned my dislike of Leecher? Not I, and especially not at Mr. Humber's inn."

"You don't say." Constable Wattersley eyed his sister rather more sharply than I thought his innocent face capable of. "Pam, where might you get that story? Is that a fact, you didn't hear Miss O'Carty make mention of this Leecher?"

I was happy to see how discomfited she looked as she confessed sulkily, "I was told it. Jolyon told me."

"Really? And who told him?" I glanced at the red-haired fellow, who seemed a bit confused, but not for long. He looked at someone behind me in the doorway, and I looked over my shoulder, to see Tod Humber standing there beside the constable, shifting from one foot to the other and looking desperately unhappy. His uncle seized the chance—or was it the truth, after all?

"Tod, tell the lady what you told me, about her friend Leecher."

"Aye," said the boy, lowering his gaze. " 'Twas me told him. He's my uncle, Miss Nona. I had to tell."

The realization that I had Tod to thank for these incredible insinuations took my breath away. I would have felt the same if he had struck me. I was both confused and depressed.

"I don't think I understand. Did this boy tell you that I was responsible for pushing Leecher off the Stones?"

By the triumphant sparkle in Jolyon Humber's still-red-rimmed eyes, I knew I had somehow played into their hands. Whenever I looked at those eyes, I remembered how they got red-rimmed from rubbing, after the powder I had thrown at him, and did not wonder at his hatred.

"Darling," Max interposed here, "it's all a trick. Don't let them lead you into a trap." He said then to the constable, "You'll find you've a liar on your hands if you mean to go by the words of that boy. From the beginning he has lied."

The constable, while not giving this much weight, was a trifle upset. "Eh? How's that, lad? Is this the truth, what you say about the man Leecher, that Miss O'Carty, in your presence, said she hated him and was glad he was dead?"

I had not said this or anything like it, I thought; yet I could not be sure. Many times since the deafness came down upon me, I had caught myself thinking aloud, not aware of it. And hadn't I really thought similar thoughts about Leecher when I found his body on the cave-ledge?

"If Miss O'Carty is accused of murdering Leecher—" Max began, to be interrupted by the constable's quickly raised hand.

"Now, sir, I never said that. You'll allow you never heard me say it."

"If so," Max went on sternly, "then you must have found his body, and I understand you have not done so."

"There *is* a body," I insisted, not liking Max's form of defense. "Tod and I found it together. How could I possibly have killed Leecher when I was with the boy all that time?"

"Until the body is found, we can't say as to that. But young Humber knows how long Miss O'Carty was with him before the discovery."

"Don't forget," Pam Wattersley reminded her brother, "Tod says he met the O'Carty woman as she was coming in off the downs."

"That is a lie," I said clearly. "Tell them so, Tod. I was coming downstairs when I met you."

Tod looked from one to the other of us. I knew he was afraid of his uncle and the company his uncle had brought, but to me the difficulty seemed to be that everything Tod knew had been twisted around until it meant the very opposite.

"But Miss Nona—I come up from the 'tater cellar, and had the slops, and you was just where you'd be if you was to come up from the downs."

Before the rest of them could make anything from this rigamarole, I said quickly, "I was at the foot of the stairs, as you remember, and we went out across the downs at once. You remember, Tod?"

"Aye, mum. That I do. It's only that we did see the body. And 'twas you that saw it, Miss."

"There's the idiot tale," cut in the blond foreigner in a brutal way. "Just so. The woman found the body for the very good reason that she put it there. That is undoubtedly why she persuaded the boy to take her there."

Max started to say something, but the constable was already putting in, with a glance at me, "We aren't at all sure there is a body. We didn't find it when we looked, Jolyon and me. There'll be an investigation, and I've a notion it's to be me that finds the body. Else there'll be more doubts cast. That's the next thing on the day's doings."

Max said abruptly. "All this is absurd. Miss O'Carty must come with me. We've an engagement in Dublin before nightfall. We'll never make it now. And further" —he and Jolyon Humber exchanged sharp looks like the *en garde* of two fencers—"Constable Wattersley is perfectly aware that I was after this Leecher in my car when he cut across the downs toward what I suppose was the group of monoliths you call the Stones. So Miss O'Carty could not possibly have killed him when I was chasing him halfway across the county."

Constable Wattersley mused over this and came up with the thoughtful and unpleasant idea, "There would still be time. If Miss O'Carty left her room immediately after you drove off in pursuit of the man. She would have to know the downs, of course."

"Which I do not," I put in.

"It fair prods me," said Pam, her thickly painted lips curling, "why none of you found the body when you searched the Stones. Where'd you say it was, Tod, exactly?"

Tod looked at me, and I nodded. Why keep that a secret, since he had blabbed everything else he knew, in such a way as to make me look at least half-guilty?

"But did you search below the Stones, sir?" The boy asked. "It was back in my cave where Miss O'Carty dragged out the body. Not proper on the Stones."

"Well, then. You see?" said the blond woman, pinching her foreign-looking, heavy-faced companion.

The constable and Jolyon Humber considered this an agreed between them that this must explain why they had not found the body when they made their search.

Tod listened to their agreements and, looking perplexed, started to say, "But Uncle, before you went out with the constable, I told you that—"

"That'll do, boy!" barked his uncle in such a way that even I, deaf though I was, could guess his command over Tod.

"Well now." Constable Wattersley looked around at all of us. "I think now we're moving. Yes. We're moving in the right way. Jolyon, we may as well get it done proper. We'll take the Land Rover and drive out. If there is a body, we'll bring it in. What do you say?"

"Agreeable," said Jolyon Humber, shrugging his big shoulders. "And my friend here, Kurt Altmann, will come along for to give us his hand to help. And Tod to show us where."

"Please, sir," Tod ventured, after looking at me in a way I did not even pretend to understand. "I been walking quite a bit. I'm that tired, I'd never make it. But I could tell you exactly where it was."

The constable nodded good humoredly. "That's as may be. If the boy gives us the directions, what's the harm if he stays in Combe until we get back with the Land Rover?"

"You may consider me his substitute," said Max, to my surprise.

Everyone looked at him. A lack of enthusiasm in that look would be putting it mildly. Only the constable welcomed him. "Good enough. May I ask why, sir?"

"I want to be quite sure that nothing is tampered with by these . . . friends of yours."

"That is your privilege, sir." And meanwhile, Miss O'Carty will be good enough to remain in one of the rooms of the hotel here and . . . and rest."

In spite of his gentle way of putting it, I knew perfectly well that I was to be hostage until they returned and found out whether, in their opinion, I was a murderess. It was preposterous, but it was also just the sort of trickery I might have expected from *them*. I could hardly wait for Scotty MacLeish to call me back and then come to Max's and my rescue.

There was somewhat more fussing about than I would have expected before they left and before I went up to the room assigned to me. Pam Wattersley and the others in that evil crew, as I thought of them, were anxious for the group to be on its way. But Constable Wattersley was not a stout man for nothing. He ordered salmon pasties prepared, and a container of "clotted," or Devonshire, cream—for what purpose I couldn't imagine—and innumerable thermoses of hot tea.

Max came and took my hands and spoke to me just before they left. "Be careful while we are gone, *Liebchen*. Don't move about alone. I don't know where the Altmann creature and his woman are going to be, but I wouldn't put anything beyond him. However, he won't dare to act against you now, while your accusations against them are fresh in this constable's mind."

"And there's that Pam Wattersley," I remarked, thinking of her vicious little smile and the way she kept looking at me as she would have looked at an insect she was about to step on. "I trust her even less. She and Humber, between them, put Tod up to all that idiocy about my killing Leecher."

Max had no use for the boy and dismissed him with a brevity that hurt me; for in spite of everything, I could not help liking Tod Humber. "A born liar, that boy! Don't get involved with him again."

He kissed my two hands as he held them in his, and then he and I kissed each other and Constable Wattersley came to us, saying briskly, "You'll like the little sitting room abovestairs, Miss. There's a good view of the downs. We shan't be more than two hours, I shouldn't think. What with that fog coming down thick as cream, we may be a trifle longer. I'm sure you've nothing to worry about, Miss. You don't look the sort who'd push a man to his death."

I thanked him, and he and Max went out to get into the Land Rover with Jolyon Humber, whose curly red hair blew wildly in the wind. I saw Tod Humber standing in the parlor, looking through the open doorway at me in the musty, cabbage-smelling little hall. He looked ashamed—as well he might. But there was also a kind of furtiveness in the way he watched the group including his uncle drive off down the curving little street and out onto the rocky lane that was hardly more than a path.

I knew exactly what they would find. It could not surprise me, I thought, and all I had to do was to wait. I still couldn't believe that anyone would be so stupid or vicious as to seriously accuse me of killing the man Leecher. But I had to be prepared for some such possibility. I half-considered calling Mother and Papa and asking them what to do about, perhaps, getting legal counsel, but I knew what would happen. Papa would throw up his job, rush out, plunder the bank account, and fly over here, where, with his hatred of the English, he would be more hindrance than help.

It was only a few hours since Miss Nettings had called Scotty MacLeish for me. Still, while I waited, I might call again, if I could get someone to help me. With Nurse Tusingham on my trail, plus those creatures who were out there now trying to involve me with Leecher's death, I didn't want to make any more mistakes. It had to be Scotty himself, next time.

I was about to ask the young clerk behind the hotel desk if he would make a trunk call for me, when I noticed the brutal-looking man and woman who had backed up Jolyon Humber. They were leaning against the far end of the desk, nearest the door. I had a pretty good notion they were there in that strategic position in order to prevent my leaving the hotel, so I turned and went up the stairs to the sitting room assigned to me.

I stood several minutes with my hand on the doorknob, wondering what I should do, how I could manage to shake off those watchdogs downstairs. I heard nothing, of course, but some sense of danger, maybe an unexpected shadow briefly crossing the light from the window, made me pivot around toward the window across the room. I could hardly believe what I saw— two hands grasping the windowsill at the side. Someone was climbing along the side of the building at least fifteen feet above the ground, obviously bent on burglary.

I stiffened to readiness, looking around for a weapon. There was a rickety chair in front of the big, old-fashioned wardrobe, and if necessary, I knew I could break that chair over the man's head and shoulders as he entered. I took up the chair, held it as a club, and tiptoed over to the window.

The hands at the window fumbled to open it, but it was locked. Then the knuckles rapped on the glass. And then, with what I expect was a very cynical laugh, I set the chair down. It was Tod Humber out there, very liable to break his neck if I didn't unlock that window.

"What on earth are you doing out there?" I asked him as I let him in.

"It's an awful day. I disremember when it was so grim," Tod remarked, and I looked beyond him at that moorland world, which was gradually falling under a peculiar pall, until, as we watched it became shrouded in that depressing and ugly yellow-brown fog.

"Never mind the weather. I nearly let you fall. I'm not at all happy about you," I told him sternly. "You lied about me to those people who are trying to kill me."

"Oh no, Miss Nona! It was true. I didn't know for sure that you hadn't come in off the downs when I saw you first at Uncle's front door."

"And I suppose you also believe I was the only person who knew where Leecher's body was."

He hesitated. "Well, I—I forgot something."

"You certainly did. You forgot that when we met

your Uncle Jolyon on the Stones you told him where we had found Leecher and he knew all about it."

He clapped his hands. "That's it, Miss. That's the very puzzler. When Uncle Jolyon said today that I'd never told him where Leecher was—that's when I knew."

"You knew?" I repeated ironically. "Then why didn't you speak up and tell the constable?"

He was very reasonable, as children always are in their arguments. "But I tried to interrupt. Didn't you notice?" He caught himself. "Beg pardon. Most like, you didn't hear. You're so sharp at guessing, Miss Nona, I forget you've the trouble. But you see, I only found out just now when they was talking down in the parlor. That was when I started to say so, when Uncle said he'd never known about the business, and I thought, all of a sudden, that what he said wasn't true at all. Then I had a better notion. So I come up here."

"Why?" I asked coldly. "You can't do me any good here." I sat down on the rickety chair and put my hands over my ears to stop the roaring, which came when I was nervous. Then I stared at him. "Why, Tod? Why? What was the point of their getting the constable to go out there now? Why not last night or at dawn? Why all the pretense?"

Tod shook himself and came over to where I sat. He looked into my face, trying very hard to make me understand the first time he spoke, as I realized, so there would be no need for a repetition. "That's what I've just thought of. Don't you see. It's not that Uncle Jolyon means to be so wicked. But he's got those awful folks over him. He must do what they say."

I didn't argue with him. He wanted to believe that. Besides, he was hurrying on. "Look now. I've thought and thought, and there's only one reason why they didn't want the constable to find the body until now. They had to—to do something to the body."

I felt sick at the ideas that ran through my mind.

"What do you mean, do something. Do what?"

"Make it look like you killed that man. Drop your handkerchief beside it. You know. Things like that."

"Don't be silly. You're imagining things. You've seen too many movies."

His eyes sparkled. "It is like that, isn't it? And now we're going to beat them, like the heroes in the flicks."

"What do you mean?"

"We must hurry." He began to shake me. "We're going to beat them. I know a path over the downs. We'll get there, and if they've put your handkerchief by the body or some-ut, we'll change it. When they get there, they won't know what to think. It'll be very funny. We'll be sitting back here in Combe Coster as innocent as can be."

He had me on my feet and was almost pushing me toward the window. I had to remind him that I seldom made either entrances or exits via second-story windows.

"Besides," I added, "in my opinion you betrayed me once. Why should I trust you now?"

"Quick." He went right on as if I hadn't said a word.

Obediently, I followed as he tugged at my arm. At the window he pointed out how he had come. There wasn't too much to do, for an active person. I've climbed a good deal more in my life than he asked me to climb then. It was merely a matter of holding on to the windowsill while making one step to the low roof adjoining; then, as Tod explained, we crossed that roof and went down an outside back staircase that was somewhat the worse for wear but had stood some hundred and fifty years in the same condition.

"Nothing to it, you see?" said Tod brightly, when I had followed his lead, climbed out, held on for dear life, and got my leg over from the sill to the roof a very long stride away. Within two or three minutes we were on the ground.

Before us spread the chalky, deserted downs. Even

while we watched, the nearest landmarks fast disappeared under the creeping yellow fog.

"Come on," Tod urged me.

I stared at him. *I don't even know if I can trust you,* I thought. *You might be the one they've selected to kill me. . . .*

Chapter Fourteen

"COME ALONG, Miss. We've no time to lose," Tod urged me.

I looked around, pretending I wanted to be sure we weren't observed by anyone. There was still that tow-haired Altmann pair who might be hanging around waiting for us to make this move. And as for the sexy Pam Wattersley, I wouldn't trust her any further than I would trust Tod's Uncle Jolyon.

Well, then, I thought, I must trust someone, and it looked as if Tod was elected. Besides, his theory about why they hadn't reported Leecher's body was a very sound one. Aside from the ridiculous stuff about their leaving one of my handkerchiefs there, which would be a little too obvious even for that crew of cutthroats, he really had a very good idea. Frightening, but sensible. They had deliberately put off the finding of the body because they wanted it found in some special way, to implicate me.

"Tod," I said as we hurried out across the fields nearest the village, "Why do you think those people want to implicate me in that man's death?"

He looked surprised, and before answering, he pointed out a slippery pool scummed over by harsh, prickly growths, weeds that were themselves coated by a chalky, dirty-white substance. "Be careful, Miss. There's places you must beware of."

"Yes, but Tod, you must have heard your uncle and that Miss Pam talking about me. I know their reason for attempting to kill me. It's something to do with politics. They are working for an enemy of Britain, and I have evidence that frightens them."

147

"What evidence?" asked Tod practically. "You mean, you have secret papers or some-ut of that sort?"

I had to smile. "No. This evidence is in my head. You see, I heard the voice of someone important in their organization as he committed a murder. And when I—" I stopped. I was beginning to doubt all the doctors' promises—it seemed so long since I had heard real sounds, not just the roaring in my ears." *"If* I ever hear again, I can testify against the guilty man."

"Bloody awful!" cried Tod, his eyes wide. Then he blushed. "Beg pardon, Miss. I never meant to say that. But this is as good as the flicks, any day."

"Not to me, it isn't," I returned grimly when I understood him. And we tramped on. As it grew chillier, the fog clinging to us with greedy fingers, I crossed my arms and slapped my shoulders to restore circulation. "You haven't told me yet what you heard about me at home. I understand about their wanting to kill me, but why should they go to the trouble of making me look like a murderess? They know perfectly well that I'd never be found guilty. It looked so like an accident, even if some people might suspect me . . . It's a silly game."

"You know what I think," Tod said after giving it consideration. "If they can get folk to thinking bad of you, then nobody'll believe you when you can hear again and you say things about their man."

What he said was mixed-up, but it made sense, and I believed that it might very well be the answer. Meanwhile, it was up to us to get to the Stones first and spoil their nasty little plan.

Tod had a real gift for pathfinding. Several times we crossed the little lane that cut more or less diagonally across the heath and that I had taken when found by Constable Wattersley, but we steered clear of the wagon trail by which Max and the others had taken the Land Rover. Once, we came close to it but avoided it neatly by creeping along beneath some heathery-looking furze or whatever the prickly hedge-road was made of.

Much before I would have expected it, we could see the monoliths looming up on the horizon, set on the tableland, which seemed higher than it was because the downs rolled away from it in all directions. I was for hurrying on faster than ever, anxious to get our dangerous and nerve-racking detective work done, but Tod stopped me suddenly. "D'you hear that?"

For a minute, under the influence of his quick, boyish tension, I too listened, unmoving. Of course, I heard nothing. "What is it? What's the matter?"

I had apparently spoken too loud, a fault of some of my ancestors, and Tod put his grubby, chalky hand over my mouth. "Sh! They'll hear!"

"Who?" I tried to look back over his hand but could see nothing. There were too many folds in the little hills, folds that had served us very well when we were trying to keep from being seen. But at the same time, they also concealed anyone who might be trailing us.

Tod mouthed unspoken words to me. "It's like something walking. Somewhere around us."

"Behind us, you mean? Trailing us?" I whispered.

He shrugged; then, after listening for interminable seconds, he shook his head. "It's like that sometimes, out here. Somebody's around. Of course," he added fairly—to soothe me, I suppose, "it's prob'ly a moor pony. They come over here from the west sometimes. Not often, though. Too much chalk here. They like it wet."

"Never mind the natural history. Is it safe to go on?"

He stuck his head out above a bush and looked around. Then he said with ludicrous disappointment, "There's a moor pony about, right enough. I can see the prints. And I thought there was going to be a bit of a dustup."

"Frankly, I'm glad there wasn't," I told him, and greatly relieved, I got up, stretched all my cramped muscles, and started rapidly on.

He kept stopping and looking around, however, trying to see his imaginary pursuers within the fog, which engulfed us now on every side. Even Tod, with his sharp vision, couldn't possibly see anyone if we actually were being followed.

"We'll be there soon," I said when his actions began to make me nervous. "And no one has bothered us yet. If they'd seen us, they'd certainly have done something before this."

"He's a quiet one," Tod murmured, coming along beside me but looking backward in the most disconcerting way.

"The moor pony?"

"Whoever it is."

It wasn't a very satisfactory answer, and I found myself beginning to look back too. We were close to the Stones, when ahead of us, a flesh-and-blood man, in a heavy macintosh and a kind of cap like a tam, obviously a villager, came down toward us, having crossed through the monoliths.

"Mr. Hawkins," Tod called to him. "Have you seen the constable or my uncle?"

"Saw a pair off yon. The Rover was stuck in a pothole. Seems like they'd all left it."

"And the other man? You said you saw only two," I said nervously.

But Mr. Hawkins didn't know anything about another man, and he passed us and soon dissolved into the misty fog, taking the big steps of a person extremely familiar with the countryside. He left Tod and me still not sure that the third man from the Land Rover had not been the one Tod heard following us.

"It's all right if it's Max," I said. "I hope it is. But if it's one of the others . . ."

With the same idea, Tod and I both began to run toward the Stones. The ground sloped upward now, and I was grateful for the covering fog, in spite of the cold and dampness. Otherwise, since it was barely two o'clock in the afternoon, we'd have been seen for miles in three directions. We clambered up the steep west side of the tableland, and Tod, getting up first, helped me by pulling me up with a hard yank.

"Now!" he said firmly. "It's got to be here, because if it isn't, then they'll call me a liar with you, Miss. Come!"

Thank heaven, we were there, at the end of our climb! I remember that curious and, in retrospect, absurd confidence I had that all would turn out right. Tod and I reached those huge, ancient creatures, the stone monoliths, and we carefully prowled over to the north end of the Stones. It was so foggy, and the fog so full of that dirty yellow mist, that we couldn't have seen shadows even if there had been any.

"My cave is over at this end. Remember?" Tod reminded me, as we tiptoed along the northern edge and peered down into the hollowed-out place where the boy and I had stumbled on Leecher's body last night. Finding the dry fountain of stone, we stepped downward with great care. I didn't want to have a fall of the sort that might have killed Leecher, whether his had been an accident or murder, and with some remaining mistrust of my companion, I let him go first.

"Guess what?" he said as I made my way down and ducked under the entrance of that hollowed-out haven in the rocks.

"Is it there?"

He moved aside cautiously, and I saw Leecher's body lying just as Tod and I thought we had left it when we pulled it back into the darkness and climbed out of this weird and ancient place.

"He looks natural, don't he?" Tod remarked, starting to investigate the body but stopping until I joined him.

"Too natural." In a gingerly way, I ran my hands over the body. "Tod, I have a nasty feeling they haven't even touched the body. We may be on a wildgoose chase."

"A what?"

"Never mind. But I can't find a thing. He's just as he was last night."

But Tod wasn't giving up that easily. "It don't seem like good sense. We must take over such care. I wonder if he carries papers."

I was angry with myself for not having thought of this. He reached into the breast of the man's waterproof while I cringed at the thought of this close proximity to a body that had been dead for at least twelve hours. Apparently Tod felt as I did, after all. He stopped and pulled his hand out, and I said encouragingly, "Try under his body."

He started to do so in a gingerly way, paused abruptly beside the man's body.

"You did find something! What is it?"

He made a face and licked his lips. I felt that he was nearly as repulsed as I was, so I reached out to the body.

"Feel," Tod said, and looked at me, repeating the word when I did not understand.

I followed his indication to the cold, curled fingers of the dead man's right hand and then jumped back. The shock was so great and so repulsive that I thought I was imagining things. I whispered, "What did it feel like to you?"

He swallowed hard. "Like as if his fingers was furry."

We looked at each other. I knew we had to do something quickly, to examine anything unusual or odd about the dead man.

"See if any of them are in sight." Then I remembered that if Tod left me for a single instant now, he might afterward be forced to admit it, and I, in turn, could be accused of tampering with evidence while he was gone. So we both got up and looked over the tall monoliths to the farther end of the Stones. There seemed to be nothing in the entire world of the downs except the thick, frightful yellow fog. Although we could see nothing, neither could anyone spying on us at that precise minute get a better view of us.

We knelt over the body of the shark-faced man

again and returned to that repulsively odd thing
clutched in the fingers of his right hand.

"It isn't fur," I said finally, having got up the nerve
to lift his hand. "It's hair. Human hair, I think."

Tod agreed. "There's a deal of hairs, like he pulled
them when he saw he was being knocked off the cliff,
or something." He looked closely at the tangle of hairs.
"They look . . . like somebody I know."

"Who?"

He stared at me, his eyes betraying what I had begun to suspect.

"It's mine, isn't it? My hair. The hair of the murderess when she pushed him over the edge of the
Stones."

"It's very like."

I began to shiver. The cold of the creeping fog had
got to me. "I suppose you think now that I really did
kill the fellow."

He bent over the dead hand, studying it with a con-
centration that would have done credit to Scotty Mac-
Leish. "No, Miss. I don't think you did it at all. You
know why?"

I shook my head.

He grinned proudly. "Because when we moved him
last night, those hairs weren't in his fingers. I felt his
fingers. Truly!"

I felt a tremendous relief.

"Oh, Tod, thank you!"

But now that we had found what we came for, Tod
was philosophical and a trifle cocky about his success.

"Well, let's have a go at the rest of him. Maybe
there's other things was put to him. We should find it
while we've the chance."

So, together, we ran our hands over the body, trying
not to look at the dead face or any part of his flesh
that was uncovered. I was the first to see the torn scrap
of paper beneath Leecher's body when we shifted him
gently. It seemed to be a couple of inches torn off a
photocopy of a letter, but there was little to go on.

"The top's gone, and the bottom, too," Tod said thoughtfully. "It's part of a letter about a female. See?" We read it together.

. . . seen last at Keswicke Corner, escaping from custody, and unreported thereafter. It is believed the intention of subject was to take up the night packet to the Republic of Ireland. In which case, Inland Revenue will be on the . . .

"That's all," murmured Tod. "Who could it be?"

But I knew at once. "It's me. And what's worse, it sounds very much as though our shark-faced friend is a detective. Otherwise, they could hardly call on Her Majesty's customs men to stop me."

Tod looked at me, obviously impressed. "You mean, Miss, the Inland Revenue and the police and Scotland Yard is all on your trail because you're a witness?"

"I'm very much afraid so." As if that wasn't bad enough, I was fairly sure this torn letter was still another bit of evidence against me in the matter of Leecher's death. "Tod! They're bound to think it was me. The letter clearly shows he was following me."

"I been givin' it a bit of a thought," Tod announced then, with his young brows knitted. "And I think they must've got that hair from combings you left in the room at Uncle Jolyon's."

I thought back to the lights and shadows in my room as Tod and I had waited in the graveyard below. "Tod! I can tell you how they found those strands of hair. It was when you went back up and brought me the contents of my purse. Remember? You met your uncle's friends in that room."

It was crushing to him to have his last faith in his uncle shattered, and very humanly, he blamed his uncle's girlfriend. "It was that Pam. She'd a deal to say to what poor Uncle Jolyon was up to." Then he quickly recovered at the thought of playing this dan-

gerous game with me against those who had let him
down.

"I could tell Constable Wattersley how it was last
night, and now today. He would not think I lied. He
likes me." Meanwhile, however, he was carefully removing the strands of hair from Leecher's fingers.

Whoever had put the combings in the dead man's
hand had been thorough, to say the least. A dozen or
more of my land hairs had been smoothed, straightened, far different from the little wad of hair I had removed from my comb and thrown automatically in the
wastebasket. These hairs, in the tight grasp of the dead
man, looked, even to me, just the way they would
look if he had grabbed his murderess by the hair as he
fell.

Thanks to Tod, we got the tangle of hairs away, and
then, while I was still debating this criminal destruction
of evidence, Tod took the piece of the letter and gave it
to me.

"We'd best be going now," he suggested, after looking up over the long stretch of frightening, haunting
monoliths that had seen so much and revealed so little,
even of their own age.

I moved away from the poor man I had been so
afraid of yesterday, and it occurred to me suddenly
that he had not known of Nurse Tusingham's treachery. If there was any possibility that she was in the
west counties last night, she might very likely have
been the murderess. I began to climb back up to the
Stones. After my unaccustomed exertions during the
past few days, I found it a good deal harder to climb
back up than it had been to slide down.

Tod leaned over the edge of the tableland excitedly.
"Hush! Constable's comin'. Uncle's with him."

I did not have time to ask myself where Max was.
I backed down to Tod's "cave" and looked around.
From here to the chalky ground did not seem too far,
but it was steep. However, if Tod and I held tight to
the spurs of rock, we could drop down and crouch

among the heathery bushes that grew in a long furrow
running slightly north and east.

Tod and I scrambled down hurriedly, Tod grinning
and mouthing to me the words, "We got it all set in
time." But aside from a fine display of nerves at the
close promimity of the law represented by Constable
Wattersley, I also felt guilty at the way we had destroyed genuine evidence together with the false.

We had no time to get farther away. The two of us
hid in the brush below, waiting for the constable and
Humber to make their discovery, which should prove
to be quite a shock to Jolyon Humber. Nervously,
I prayed for a renewal of those great, evil puffs of yellow fog. If they became just a bit thicker, I felt, Tod
and I would be much safer hurrying away from this
spot, following the hollows as we had last night. The
longer we had to wait here, the greater likelihood there
was of our being discovered by the two up there on the
Stones.

As we crouched there behind those sharp, dry bushes,
our feet and legs covered with blown dust, I felt almost
at my lowest ebb. The moment came when I saw
Jolyon Humber and Constable Wattersley gesticulating, evidently talking loudly. And although I could
hear nothing, I knew that everything they said was a
danger to me.

My heart nearly stopped when Humber, standing
with legs apart, seemed to survey the whole area where
Tod and I were hidden. Then he pointed a long,
brawny arm directly at Tod and me and yelled something. I did not move. Then I felt a stir beside me. Tod
was getting up.

"No—no. Please don't!" I whispered, as I realized he
must be about to betray me, but he did not hear me, or
if he did, he ignored it. I covered my face. I felt as if
everything had come to an end. The silence was louder
than ever.

Chapter Fifteen

I FELT Tod leave me, stumbling a little as he got around the brushwood. I looked up. Although I could hear nothing, I began to understand what had happened. Tod's uncle must have caught a glimpse of his nephew, and he was apparently demanding that Tod come out and show himself. The boy, seeing that the game was up, had cleverly and bravely come out, pretending to be the only person hiding there. I watched him now, full of admiration for the way he went up to the Stones, scuffing his feet, showing the greatest reluctance but with deliberate intention, I felt sure. I wondered if I should come out and show myself, taking some of the onus of his guilt in his uncle's eyes by making it seem that it was my idea. But I knew that the constable could have no thought that the boy had destroyed evidence, whereas I, after Humber's accusations, might be in a much different situation.

By the time Tod reached the steep little ascent of that tableland where the monoliths were, Constable Wattersley and Humber were examining the body of the dead Leecher.

When Tod scrambled up the side to his little cave and joined the men, I waited stiffly to see if the boy would betray me. He did not. His uncle made as if to give him a terrible wallop across the head, but he ducked, and at the same time the constable said something, evidently to interfere.

I saw Tod ask a question, and the Constable replied, shaking his head. Tod turned around and stared out at the drifting fog banks a little beyond me. He pretended to hold out his hand and feel for rain, as the air was growing misty. But I felt sure he was trying to tell me something. Then I saw his big, toothy grin and the odd way he pointed to his mouth. I knew then he must be pantomiming pleasure, and at this minute, the only pleasure he and I shared must be that the constable had found no evidence. The body was just as it had been when they first murdered Leecher. There was no more planted evidence.

My reading of that smile must have been correct, because very shortly the constable was making gestures, and he and Jolyon Humber began to pull the body out. I was startled when, almost immediately, the constable's Land Rover came rattling and bumping over the downs to the foot of the Stones. Max was driving it. He leaped out, and I could see that he was furious. He had that scowl which always meant trouble. Probably it had been decided, over his strong objections, that he should get the Land Rover to working again, while the other two men went over the downs on foot. Tod started to scramble down to Max but was restrained by his uncle.

Max called up to the constable, who shook his head and then went on working on the body, with Humber's assistance. I suspected that Tod wanted to tell Max where I was, but at the moment the boy was called on to help remove the body. And with the securing of ropes to the closest stone monolith and the wrapping of the body in an improvised shroud of bedsheets, they managed to get poor Leecher down into the Land Rover.

By the time they had settled matters, there was an argument between Max and the constable. I had an idea Max wanted to walk. They were still discussing whatever it was, in the crowded Rover, when they drove off. Max looked back, almost to where I was, and leaped over the side of the Rover and started to walk. I hoped very much that he would come back in my direction, back past the Stones, but he did not, and I could not come out of my hiding-place until the constable was out of sight. I saw then that Max was heading southwest across the downs toward the village, and it occurred to me that he was hurrying back to be with me and tell me they had found nothing incriminating against me. He would know how anxious I was.

Max's figure in its dark coat seemed to appear and then vanish several times, in and out of the dirty fog, which was now fast turning to mist. I came out from my hiding-place in a gingerly way, looking around but unable to make out anything moving in all that misty fog. Still, if only I had had enough energy to run from this spot to the point at the southeast corner of the Stones, I would have reached the point where I saw Max swallowed up for the last time in that persistent shroud of bad weather.

I started fast, then had to slow as my shoes sank in chalky deposits. Even so, it was hardly two minutes before I reached the place where Max had jumped out of the Rover and started striding on the shortcut across the downs to Combe Coster. I ran a short distance, persistently walking out of my shoes, which kept sticking in the soil in such obstinacy that I wanted very much to scream. I thought it possible that either the mist would thin out or I would make out Max's figure in the distance as he strode over the crest of the rolling downs, but neither happened.

He must be walking even faster than I had supposed, unless he had got turned about and gone in quite a different direction, and that wasn't a bit like the capable Max Brandt that I had come to know. I could see nothing beyond the vague, unreal humps of earth in any direction with the single exception of the great stone monoliths, now behind me. I wondered if I had better wait here. Tod was sure to come back, knowing that the area was strange to me. Or if he did not come, he would tell Max, providing he trusted him, and then Max would return.

I ran on a litle way toward the southwest, which I thought was the way to Combe Coster. I have always had a good head for directions and felt sure I was not mistaken this time. But the cold was bone-chilling, and my shoes, of course, were never meant for this sort of cross-country race. When I stopped in a deep vale between the hills and brushed dust and dirt off my foot before tripping back into the shoe, my fingers seemed stiff as wood. I put them nearly to my mouth—they were terribly dirty—and blew on them hard.

I had the most curious sensation. I actually heard . . . or maybe I only imagined I heard . . . the sound of my own breath exhaled! I straightened, sat very still, and listened. Now there was nothing again, only that roaring in my head which seemed to have been my companion since the dark moment in Mr. Putney's stationer's shop. Yet just for a few seconds, I had really seemed to hear.

There had been a sound! And it was a different sound from that which I'd become used to. If this proved to be true and my hearing came back, even intermittently, then of course, I must return to London and be shut up in Scotty's precious "hospital" or some similar prison-like place so that I could help to identify the murderer's voice when the man was located. But to do all this, I had to get safely back to Combe Coster. It horrified me to think how quickly Jolyon Humber and the rest would act, once they found I had moments during which I could hear—since I had no doubt at all that they were acting on orders from Nurse Tusingham, my real and basic enemy.

I stamped my stockinged foot into my shoe, and with a groan or two at the ache in my ankles and all the muscles of my legs, I staggered up and started out. At first, I took quick steps, close to a jogtrot, hurrying along what I thought of as a trench in the hills. This became a run, and still it seemed to me that it was longer than ever, before I was out of sight of the Stones. During this time, upon several separate occasions I was overcome by the sensation that I heard different noises, not the sounds that had filled my ears and my mind during the past week or so, but new sounds—the moan-

ing noise of the wind, the faint splatter of the mist upon any exposed object, and then, after some minutes, the falling away of earth and sand under heavy footsteps.

That was ridiculous. I was absolutely alone out on the downs. I stopped and looked around, just to satisfy this peculiar sensation of mine. There were odd noises, nature's sounds, that I heard in little snatches now, but in between there was the old roaring silence, and I wasn't absolutely sure that I hadn't imagined the rest. I stood on tiptoe and looked along the tiny valley I was following, between the hills that rolled away into what I thought of in those moments as an eternity of fog and mist.

When I climbed a few steps up the side of one of those little hills, I could better make out objects in the near-distance. I was surprised to find there really was a four-footed animal, a moor pony, wandering about at the foot of the Stones, which still loomed behind me. Tod had heard the pony an hour or two before, and now I could just make out the shaggy little creature enjoying a dry meal off the ground I had just passed. I had a strong feeling of sympathy for him. He was out of his element, just as I was out of mine. I glanced around once more, making out objects here and there on the horizon, only faintly discernible through the mist. Other animals probably, but impossible to see clearly.

It must be later in the day than I had thought. My watch said three-ten o'clock, but it looked dark enough to be later. The mist had slackened, but the fog was dirtier and thicker than ever. I looked out across that long, unmarked path back to Combe Coster, and I knew I hadn't the faintest idea how to find it beyond the general southwesterly direction. I had already run for nearly half an hour and still wasn't sure I was running toward the village itself. I had certainly lost hope of catching Max before he reached the village or before Tod told him where he had left me.

I walked for ten minutes more, decided I had been going west instead of in a southerly direction, and gave up. I sat down abruptly on top of one of those endless hills, and shielding my eyes from the yellow glare, I tried to decide the best direction to take. It was confusing especially when I began to hear those imaginary sounds again, now the faint crunch of footsteps somewhere close by.

Are they real sounds this time? I thought. *Are they sounds like the moor pony . . . or someone else, close by—someone human?*

I studied the near horizon, as much of it as I could make out, although it was impossible to see anything in those little valleys between the higher rises that looked like sea waves, one very like the next. Then at a distance, perhaps a half mile to the south, I saw something that looked like a red or brown beetle, which must be a car. I was delighted. At least it was not the Land Rover, which I must avoid. If Tod had spoken to Max in town, then it was conceivable that this was Max's little red MG. Even if it wasn't, a car driven by any stranger would be a blessing to me now.

I waved, jumped up and down, did all I could to attract the attention of the occupant of the car. Then I ran along the ridge of the hill in that direction. I was still running, when I tripped over some object silently thrown in my way. Then, as I went down, falling hard to my knees, the sky seemed to collapse on me and I found myself coughing and struggling as enormous folds of cloth dropped over me and then tightened . . . tighter . . . I was strangling. I struggled like a wildcat, scratching, clawing.

And then, miraculously and in one single second, it all stopped. I had not yet lost consciousness, and my mind still functioned well enough to tell me that my attacker had been disturbed suddenly. I knew this was my hope. I relaxed and went limp, hoping my attacker would believe his job done. Whatever it was, I felt the creature leave me.

Still stifled by the hideous, smothering folds of cloth, I was vaguely aware that I heard sounds in the distance, a confusion of noises. I became so frantically busy trying to throw off the thing that had fallen over me that I found myself rolling a few feet down the hillside, during which time the noises I had heard faded under the old and now familiar roaring that I had heard intermittently since the shot was fired in Mr. Putney's shop. I managed to scramble free and blink as I saw the foggy light once more. At my feet, and billowing under the fog-laden breeze, was a common bedsheet, which would have been my shroud.

I still could not quite imagine what had happened or where my attacker had gone. It seemed obvious though, that one of those from Jolyon Humber's crowd of cutthroats had thrown that cloth over me and then tried to strangle me with a horribly adequate bit of exceedingly thin clothesline, through the folds of the bedsheet. I wondered what had stopped him, until I saw something shimmering a short distance down the next little vale below my own hill. This was the ancient, beat-up little British car I had seen some minutes before, and it was chugging along toward me for all it was worth. The unseen driver waved a hand out the open window and probably yelled. I could not tell.

I began to stumble down toward him, crying out, "Come quickly, please! Are you from the village? Please hurry." I had some notion that whoever was in the car might help me to locate the man who attacked me. He couldn't be far away.

The car came to an abrupt halt below me, and the door swung open.

Two men rushed toward me from the little car, and when I saw Max, I thought in those first few seconds that I had never been so glad to see him, nor loved him so much. But as I ran toward him and his companion, who had likewise hurried toward me, my attention was divided. The driver of the faded little English sedan was Detective Inspector Scotty MacLeish.

I slowed as I reached the foot of the hill, aware that I was scared to death, frantically nervous. And while all my sensual feelings drew me to Max, the sight of dear old Scotty comforted me no end.

I let Max grab me and hold me to him so tightly that I gasped for breath, complaining, "He's still around . . . tried to strangle me." But my complaint was to Scotty, who reached for my free hand and squeezed it gently as if to offer his unspoken sympathy.

I knew that the men must be speaking over my head, although I could not make out anything but a blurred jangle of sound. Nevertheless, it was enough to encourage me enormously. I almost told them this one piece of news, that I suspected there was a slow return of my hearing. But first, the most important fact.

With Max's fingers closed in a warm, protective embrace upon my neck the manner that had first made me love him, I said to Scotty, "Please look around, right away. One of those people who want to kill me—he tried just a few minutes ago. He might still be in sight."

Scotty started off on the run, with his hand loosely touching the breast of his macintosh. I found myself wondering if he did such a melodramatic thing as carry a gun under the flap of that breast pocket.

Without releasing me from his warm, comforting touch, Max looked around, over my head, his eyes hard as I first saw them, his lips set harshly, the network of lines in his face pointing up what another woman might have called his ugliness. I was surprised when his free hand took me by the chin so that I could see him as he said with a gentleness I sensed and almost heard, "My brave little girl. . . . Don't cry. Don't cry."

Until then, I hadn't been aware that I was crying. Ashamed of this weakness, which I impatiently blamed on my recent fright, I managed with reasonable coherence to explain how near I'd come to being strangled

Scotty MacLeish was back by that time and heard the details. We looked at him. I could guess his failure by his disgust. His reaction reminded me of Max—

there was a tight, tense look on his normally pleasant face. "He can't have come this way. Either Max or I would have seen him."

I had a sudden idea. "Yes, but if you two came from the southwest, he could have run down that hill and toward the west."

Scotty shook his head. "Unlikely. Then Max would have caught him."

I glanced at each of them in turn, not understanding. For a moment I had a prickly feeling that Max had not meant to correct my original mistake in thinking they had come together. Then, as Scotty looked at him, vaguely surprised at the silence, I supposed, Max said brusquely, "The Humber boy told me he'd left you at the Stones. I was coming out to get you when I saw MacLeish's car heading up from the southwest."

"The truth is," put in Scotty with a smile, "he was taking such long steps I nearly let him walk. Thought he'd do better than he could with me."

So they'd hadn't been together the entire distance! The thought disturbed me. "Where on earth did you two meet?" I asked, trying with difficulty to make the question light and casual.

Scotty pointed with equal casualness at a point within our own view and not far from the place where I had first seen his car. I refused to think further along this line. My throat hurt, my head felt as if it would burst, and I had one desire—to get away from this dreadful sea of chalky downs and yellow fog.

"It looks like the end of the world," I said, so suddenly that both men were startled and then exchanged glances, and Max made some suggestion, pointing to the car. I agreed in haste, although I guessed from the way Scotty took a last look around that he would rather have stayed and hunted down my attacker.

He did go back and pick up the sheet and the very thin line that had been used in the attempt to strangle me. Then, frightened and uneasy as I was, I went to

sleep in the car between Max and Scotty and didn't wake up until we reached the hotel in Combe Coster.

I was dead tired and made no objection when Max insisted that I was in no condition to talk to several frightening strangers, two men and a woman, who said they represented various aspects of the press. I hadn't the vaguest desire to give any interviews, but it was shocking to find out that a rumor had swept Combe Coster and brought those reporters to the village. Nona O'Carty, it appeared, was wanted in some connection with murder. I got the strong impression that I was considered to be the chief suspect and for that reason was currently in custody of an inspector who had come all the way down from London to apprehend me. I was too tired to get my Irish up and tell off these idiots, and I was grateful to Constable Wattersley, who effectively did this for me. I'm sure he felt the whole thing was a reflection on him. He was not in a very good mood toward me anyway; he had discovered that I had been out on the Stones, and although he did not accuse me to my face, I felt sure he was suggesting to Scotty that I might have falsified some evidence in connection with the dead Leecher.

In the hotel as Max examined my throat and treated it, I remember wondering if Scotty had sent Leecher to pick me up that day, and therefore, if Scotty had known that I suspect Nurse Tusingham as one more detestable member of Jolyon Humber's gang. At any rate, when I asked Max if Scotty suspected also that I had falsified evidence and had actually killed Leecher, he dismissed this with an angry, "Don't be ridiculous! Why would you have killed the fellow?" I was sure Max was in for a bad time with Scotty, too, when they got me out of the way. Scotty could hardly forgive this foreign-born man who had pretended to assist Scotty's department and then snatched up their only witness. But I was really too shaky and tired to worry about their problems at the moment.

One of the chambermaids helped me to take off my

coat, suit, and shoes, after which I lay down in my slip, took the capsule Max gave me, and went off to sleep, with Max, Scotty, and the constable promising to remain within call in the old-fashioned parlor that opened off the bedroom they had loaned me.

I awoke briefly late in the day, about twilight, I think, although my watch had stopped. The room was shadowy, not quite dark, yet too dark to see anything clearly. There was a steady drone from somewhere, and I listened, first casually, wishing the little noise would cease, then thinking in a confused state of half sleep, *I suppose they are discussing the murder and whether they can return me to their precious hospital in London. They probably never will capture the murderer of Mr. Putney, so how can they use me for identification?*

I closed my eyes, dazed and dreaming because of the capsule Max had given me, as I thought.

At any rate, I told myself, *it won't be too difficult for me to identify him if they ever do capture the fellow, because his voice was very much like one of those voices I hear now.*

With all my bones and muscles aching, my throat now tight and hurting me when I swallowed, I let myself drift off to sleep again, aware, however, that something had happened to me, something that my fuzzy brain couldn't concentrate on now. . . .

Chapter Sixteen

THE EVENING was well along when I began to come out of that daze and euphoria which had blocked for a few hours the pain, uncertainty, and fright that filled my waking hours. Before I opened my eyes I was momentarily troubled by the conflict of sounds and silence I fancied I heard everywhere around me.

I remember thinking, *What a vivid dream! The rain in London yesterday. Today the royal wedding. But when did the terrible thing happen in Mr. Putney's shop? And Max! He can't have been a dream. Not Max. Surely not Max. . . .*

The drone of voices and then little hollows of silence aroused me to an awareness of my surroundings. My eyes snapped open, and I sat up, wide-awake. The worn drapes had not been pulled over the window, and little lights from the main street of the village gave some illumination to the room. At least, I could make out the silhouettes of the furniture, the unlighted fireplace on the opposite wall, and beside it, the door to the parlor beyond.

A streak of light outlined the door on three sides. The wood must be warped, I thought, and then corrected myself. I must think of places like this as "historic" and "quaint." Besides, it had been exceedingly comfortable after the horrors of the day on the chalky downs. The muffled conversation that I heard so indistinctly must be coming from there. Then I saw that the door was closed, but still I heard voices. They seemed closer now and then; their direction seemed to be near the fireplace.

So now I could hear. That would make Scotty Mac-

Leish and the British police awfully happy. It would delay—heaven knew how long!—my flight with Max, and
probably my voyage home. Since it might take months
before they produced the murderer of Mr. Putney, a
man whose voice I could definitely identify, I found myself fighting off a thought that had very little civic vir-
tue in it but a lot of selfish practicality. I might pretend
I had not got my hearing back. I was still deaf, and
might always be so!

Of course. The ideal solution. I was still deaf. That
would solve everything. It would be hard to keep pretending, but it was better than being stuck away in
London for an indefinite period while creatures like
Nurse Tusingham and Jolyon Humber and his crowd
took turns trying to stab me or strangle me.

I was about to plump up the pillows and try to get
a little more sleep before making that decision about
the return of my hearing, when, quite clearly, I
heard a male voice speaking in a North-of-England accent, a musical, with a slight, indefinable difference
from a Yorkshireman movie actor I knew back home.
The difference was something I couldn't make out, an
accent acquired, probably unconsciously, upon another original dialect, I thought. And then, the realization came. What incredible luck! This was the voice
I had heard in Mr. Putney's shop, the voice of the
murderer. And since I heard it here, it must belong to
one of those creatures who had hounded me and nearly
killed me—Jolyon Humber or the blond, mean-looking
foreigner in all likelihood. After all, they were the two
men that Tod and I had seen returning from the Stones
last night. Undoubtedly, one or both of them had killed
Leecher.

". . . You know nothing of the matter," said the
voice of the man who had murdered Mr. Putney. I
traced the sound now to the acoustics of that unused
flue in the fireplace. That well-remembered musical
lilt went on, and I listened, breathless with the knowledge. "From the beginning, you have behaved stupid-

ly. The fact that I did not warn you of Tussey is not my affair but yours. And then—worse and worse. These terrors. Idiocies! One would think the girl was surrounded by monsters! It was no very persuasive method, I can tell you."

That mention of "the girl" jerked me to an awareness of my own immediate danger. I scrambled out of bed and in stockinged feet hurried to the fireplace and stuck my head in, gazing up the chimney, which, of course, was black as soot. Obviously, the voice came from someone who had access to a fireplace that shared this chimney.

So it must be next door in the parlor, so close that if he chose, the murderer might have entered this bedroom and killed me while I slept, any time during those past four hours. I thought how horrible it would be now, to walk into that room, to hear the voice, and not to betray myself. Until I could speak in private to either Max or Scotty, I dared not let anyone guess my knowledge.

A door slammed in the parlor. I guessed that it was the hall door and that someone had left the room, because there was a prlonged silence after that. It was terrible to me to consider that Scotty and the constable, men I knew and liked, and Max Brandt, the man for whom I cared most deeply, should be there in that parlor or very near; and yet I was afraid to go into the room, for fear my face and my own uneasiness would betray what I knew about one of the men who was with them.

Voices spoke in the distance. Doors opened and closed. But I did not again hear the murderer's distinctive accent.

I stayed in the dark leaning against the parlor door a few minutes, wondering what to do, how to keep up my pretense of deafness until I could get Max and Scotty alone. Meanwhile, a voice in the parlor started to speak, and as I was extremely conscious of tones and accents now, I guessed from my Hollywood studio ex-

perience that this speaker's accent was either Welsh or
at least, and most naturally, from one of the west
counties.

"I'll be saying a thing of the Londoners. They come
tight-mouth and tight-fist and leave me but the half a
tale of what's been and done."

"Ever the same, lad. Ever the same. It's the high-
and-mighty Londoners when the great things get doing.
Not us. They be none caring for us but to make us
fetch and carry."

"Now, Jol, you're bitter, lad. You never got your
due in the Blitz. We all know that. If you'd had your
due they'd have knighted you, so they would. But the
world's not got its dues. Not yet."

The word "Jol" aroused me to the point where I
tried the doorknob as gently as possible, seeing it
move under my fingers silently until the door opened an
inch at a time. I thought I could risk two inches without
the men in that room suspecting that the door was not
simply ajar. I was startled when a woman's voice spoke
up suddenly, quite close in front of the door where I
stood.

"Well, now, Jol, luv, tell my dull brother you're to
go to London yourself, soon's that precious murderess
is settled. That little Irish colleen! Very like she's a spy
for the Russkies, along of all else!"

Considering that this woman, obviously Pam Wattersley, from her conversation, was one of the gang that
Scotty called *"Them,"* I thought she was probably ac-
cusing me of the crimes in which she herself was concerned. I was sure that the man she and Jol Humber
were speaking to must be Constable Wattersley. Poor
fellow! Practically surrounded by traitors and murderers, and there he sat, trying to tell the vicious Jolyon
Humber that he should have been decorated for hero-
ism during the war! I wished very much that I could
march into that room and blurt out all the truth to
Constable Wattersley, but I did not care to until I knew
exactly whose voice I had heard earlier and recognized

as that of the murderer of the little stationer in Richmond.

There was a commotion out in the street. It was either excessively noisy or, I, with my newly regained hearing, was more than ordinarily conscious of the disturbance. Thankful for my stockinged feet, I tiptoed across the room and looked out. I was terribly relieved to see Max and Scotty surrounded by several people who did not look like townsmen and whose persistence made me suspect they were reporters. Scotty was easygoing with them, as I would have expected, but Max used a couple of angry chopping gestures that made the woman and one of the men duck to avoid him. Scotty said something to Max, probably in reprimand, and the two came across toward the hotel.

I was just beginning to wish I could have heard this exciting controversy, when I saw something that made me clutch the windowsill in panic. Across the little curving main street was a big woman in one of those nun-like habits which would always remind me of Nurse Tusingham. Then the woman started across after Scotty and Max. The quaint little streetlamp illuminated her face, and I knew beyond doubt that she was Bertha Tusingham.

Part of my mind kept asking, *Now what shall I do?* I had to get Scotty and Max alone before speaking to them. It seemed to me that every minute of my life here in Combe Coster produced more enemies, and I had got to the point where I felt I could not trust anyone here, even the constable, because they were all allied together, probably from birth. And yet it was even possible that Scotty would not believe me when I persisted in warning him not only about the voice I had heard—obviously that of someone he knew or had seen here —but also about Nurse Tusingham. I tried to think whether I had warned Max already about the treachery of his nurse. I must have, for he knew I had leaped out of that big black Rolls and run away.

Watching both Scotty and Max pause momentarily in

the street as Nurse Tusingham joined them, I didn't
know what to think. It occurred to me that Max might
be making a pretense of trust in the woman, for some
strategic reason that he would explain later. And Scotty
very possibly knew nothing of my feelings against the
nurse. I could hardly interfere publicly in whatever
secret government plans Scotty and Max were following. But as I watched the two men pause and give some
attention to Nurse Tusingham's greeting or whatever,
I could not help feeling terribly uneasy, for fear the
only two people I trusted should still believe in that
woman.

The voices in the parlor cut into my consciousness.
I recognized the peculiar twang that was Pam Wattersley's, now deep and now high-pitched as she made
a fuss over some payment of money. "Jolyon, it was
your word on it. Never you mind what for. I've not a
brother who's constable here for nothing, eh, luv?"

"If you be owing of twenty pounds to my sister,"
said Constable Wattersley, "so long as it's honest come
by, you'd do well to pay it, Jolyon lad. And that I do
say. No matter if I've the law by me or no. But mind,
Pam. You'll swear now you had no part in the death of
the city man, eh?"

"What d'you take me for?" said his sister with all the
indignation of the born liar. "You know well it was
that deaf creature's work. She's said she hated the man.
Even to Tod she said it."

But her brother countered stoutly, for which I was
better pleased with him, "How you do run on, Pam!
We've no proof yet he didn't slip and fall—outlander
as he was. Now then, I think you'd best be off, you and
Humber. The lass is that taken with fear of you, she's
like to be put off the truth all over again if she finds you
here when she wakes. And Detective Inspector Mac-
Leish and I have a deal to say to her. Private-like."

I heard a stir of chairs and could just see Pam and
Humber get up. Humber headed for the door while the

sexy brunet turned and spoke to her brother in parting, with the most sarcastic turn of voice.

"Well then! It's the noble detective inspector we must all boot-lick now. The good, the simple, the very high-and-mighty MacLeish!" And she went out after Humber, slamming the door.

I did not wonder at her dislike of Scotty, since he was the one authority who, in the general course of things, would outrank her brother, despite the constable's local power. And for this reason, I felt I could not trust Constable Wattersley or anyone liable to be swayed by the beauteous Pam and local prejudice.

When I looked out the window once more, I was too late to see what had happened to Max, but Scotty and Nurse Tusingham were still on the street, headed for the hotel's little front door. At sight of the big woman taking her mannish strides, I had the most awful notion. What if Bertha Tusingham really was a man? And if she was, she was the most logical candidate for the murderer I had overheard in Mr. Putney's shop.

The street of the little country town was now deserted so far as I could see, although some sort of wrangle was going on in front of the hotel, which I couldn't quite see. Then a flash went off, and glass spattered on cobblestones. I guessed that a photographer had taken a picture and someone, probably Max, had struck either a camera or a flashgun. *Oh, Max, be careful!* I prayed. Even as a lowly secretary in Hollywood I knew the value of good-will where the press was concerned.

Then there were footsteps over the aging board floor of the parlor, and I heard Constable Wattersley's voice close in front of my door.

"Inspector? A bit late for Combe Coster. We're not for London hours down here. And as well, if you be asking. The daylight's the best of it. But come in. And the good nurse? Come to help the poor lass, I've no doubt. Young Miss is still sleeping."

Come to help me! Very likely!

I rushed to the bed and hurried into my suit skirt and blouse, without taking time to find my shoes or comb my hair. Then, taking a deep breath in the vain hope of slowing my excited pulsebeat to something near normal, I walked across the floor, letting creak where it would, and pushed open the door into the parlor. Scotty and the constable stood, obviously surprised at my sudden appearance, and Nurse Tusingham laned forward in her detestably unctuous way.

Above all, I must remember—*I could not hear*.

I tried, deliberately, to close out all sounds, to concentrate upon the lips of the speaker, as I had during past weeks—and as before, I would frequently have to ask the speaker to repeat his words.

Scotty spoke to me. "Better, I hope, Nona. You have more color. You didn't look too rosy this afternoon."

I felt a surprising relief at the timbre, the accent of his voice, which was ordinary, pleasant, middleclass English. I realized that though I had never admitted it to myself, there must have been a tiny suspicion all this while that anyone I met since the morning of the royal wedding might speak with the murderer's voice. And I would not know. Until this minute.

I was facing Scotty when he took my hands and then said to Constable Wattersley, with the smile I remembered so well, "I would not question your authority in any way, Constable, but you do see the absolute innocence of Miss O'Carty? We simply must have her back in London for purposes of identification. And the sooner we are on our way, the better."

I looked from him to Constable Wattersley and back, as though he and the Constable spoke too rapidly for me to understand, but in the midst of this pretending, and while I tried hard to catch everything that was said, Nurse Tusingham leaned over Scotty and whispered something. Scotty nodded, glancing at the constable, whose chubby face looked a little huffy at this slight.

As the nurse left, relieving that prickle of uneasi-

ness at my back, Scotty explained. "I've sent Tusingham down to help Doctor Brandt relieve us of those journalists."

"Just so," said the constable, mofiled. "Just so."

As for me, I looked after the departed nurse and recalled that I had not yet heard her speak. I wondered about that. Whatever sex the hard-faced mannish creature was, she fitted in every way the pattern of that murderer whose identity, more than his actual existence, had hounded me every minute of every day and night since the shot in Mr. Putney's shop made its near miss. Everything terrible that had happened to me I associated, in some part, with Nurse Tusingham, even the horrors of Combe Coster. I hated and feared that creature.

I said to Scotty, "Thank you for not being angry. I knew it was stupid of Max and me to run away. It was my fault. I would have gone alone and Max knew it. But you see, I thought I would never . . ." I looked at the constable, who was stiffly attentive, not missing a word. It was unfortunate that he was so closely allied to the crowd at the Humber Inn. I finished quickly, "I thought I would never hear again, and maybe I won't."

"Of course not. I haven't known Max all these years for nothing. He was always dependable. . . . Nona, look at me when I speak to you, my dear girl."

"Yes. I'm so sorry." I caught myself just before I added, "I heard a voice in the hall exactly like Mr. Putney's murderer." By the greatest luck, I stopped myself in time. But the truth was, I really had heard the distinctive voice outside the door. When Scotty, looking behind me at the opening door, said, "Ah, Miss Tushingham, I see you've rescued our Max," I knew, for several seconds, that I had been right in suspecting Bertha Tusingham, the so-called nurse, for this voice, with the peculiar musical lilt of the murderer, was speaking now.

"I'm afraid it will mean two new cameras, but it was worth every shilling."

I was afraid to look around, for fear the "nurse" would read my recognition of that voice. I was frantic to get Scotty and Max alone, to tell them the ugly, shocking truth.

Meanwhile, Scotty laughed, in spite of an obvious effort to appear disapproving.

"Spare me your details. I know absolutely nothing, and I prefer to know even less. There may be difficulties in London. However! Constable Wattersley, I'll ask your permission to remove Miss O'Carty to London tomorrow."

Max came up behind me, and as I turned, shaken by the thought of my proximity to Nurse Tusingham, Max kissed me and shook his head at Scotty's suggestion.

As I stared at him, surprised at his contradiction of Scotty, he looked into my face as he always did when speaking to me, and I knew he would say that he wished to take me back himself. But as he spoke, I felt as though I had gone back into one of those wild nightmares in which Max spoke to me with the murderous Tusingham's north country voice.

"Nona, you know we must go back now, don't you? We must let them decide in London what is to be done, since you clearly cannot identify their precious murderer until you regain your hearing. It's no use our running to the ends of the earth. Much better to settle it one way or the other. I'll take you back. You need not go with the others if you don't wish to."

He spoke distinctly as he always did with me; yet because of my awful confusion, the reality being so much worse than anything I had suspected, I must have looked as though I did not make out what he said. He repeated it in substance, all the while that I stared at him, at all the dear things about his face that I had grown to know and trust and love. He cupped my chin with his hand now and gently rubbed it with his thumb in a way that would have been enchanting

an hour before, even a moment before I recovered my hearing.

Max, Max . . . not you. Please don't let it be you. I love you so much. How can I betray you?

His dear, loving gesture only made worse what I must do.

Chapter Seventeen

SCOTTY SAID quietly, "Oh, I think not, Max. You really are in for a bit of trouble, you know. Kidnapping a Crown witness. Well, I mean to say!"

Even now I found myself defending this strange man, my nemesis, my assassin, my love. "But it wasn't kidnapping. How could it be? I made him take me."

Constable Wattersley looked at each of us, hesitant, considering, I'm sure, the effect of all this on his own authority, but Scotty handled him tactfully, pointing out the credit that would redound to him for having located me.

"Who really was that man Leecher who died out on the Stones?" I asked, not caring at all. Anything to delay the betrayal of Max Brandt, I thought, knowing quite well that I should be reporting the truth to Scotty MacLeish at this minute.

"Leecher was a spy," Scotty explained, somewhat to my surprise. I wondered if he meant that Leecher was a government spy, but apparently not.

The constable nodded wisely, beginning to make plans for departure, which I dreaded to see, for it brought me closer to the revelation I must face. "Just so," he agreed. "There's been security leaks in the west counties. Not two months gone by, there was a dustup over some information out of Salisbury Plain that got across the Irish Channel and then to another power. About a new aircraft, it was. Leecher very likely was spying about our own little chalky Stonehenge, when he slipped. But we're not quite so grand as the great Stonehenge. We've nothing of a Crown secret out on

179

our little downs. We're not likely to attract spies and such."

I thought of Jolyon Humber and the others at his inn and would have liked to contradict the good constable in his innocence, but anything involving his own sister was sure to be bitterly resented and contested by him. And the important information I possessed must be given to Scotty first, and alone. I could not afford to let the constable, with the weight of his official status, cancel out all I had observed, including the menace of Jolyon Humber and his "guests." It was very possible that Constable Wattersley himself, with his blind faith in his sister's friends, had testified to the innocence of Combe Coster in the relaying of information to foreign powers.

Nurse Tusingham, whom I hated now because she was not the murderer instead of Max, noticed my exceedingly odd behavior and said in her annoying, intimate way, "Dearie, I must say, you haven't done yourself a bit well by running away. You needn't be frightened of us, you know."

Her comment made everyone look at me.

"*Liebchen,* you still look very pale," Max said, studying my face with that concern and apparent love with which he twisted all my feelings—hoping, no doubt, that if I did learn to hear again, I would adore him too much to betray him. Now that I heard the German endearment spoken aloud, I knew why it had always seemed to me that the murderer's accent of northern England overlaid another and older accent, his native tongue.

I smiled, with the greatest effort I have ever used, for I had not stopped loving him merely because he was what he was. But though I still cared for him, I could not forget that he was the creature I had feared all my waking hours during my period of living in constant silence.

"I'm hungry," I excused myself, and quickly, before I could change my mind, I seized this chance to tell

Scotty the truth and put the awful business in his hands. Perhaps, in his kindness to me, and his liking for Max, he might find some way to mitigate the report of the crime. "Max, could you order me up something light? Scrambled eggs and tea or something?"

Max shrugged and said with amusement, "Something light? I'd as soon eat fish and chips, for all their grease. However!" He looked around, then saw what I had known all along. There was no telephone in this room. He would have to go downstairs to order my meal.

I hated myself for the deception when I saw him go. And then, so soon after, Constable Wattersley was on his way, and I had only to get rid of Bertha Tusingham before destroying Max. For the hundredth time in as many seconds I wished that the unique voice I had heard in Mr. Putney's shop had been Nurse Tusingham's.

I looked at the stiff coif and the knowing eyes with something very close to hate, and was shaken by Scotty's perceptiveness when he suggested suddenly, "I'm sure you'll know better than Max what would be good for Miss O'Carty at this hour. Why don't you run along and help him? I'll try to guard the little lady and see that she doesn't make some spectacular escape." He smiled at me as he said this, but though I returned his smile faintly and with effort—for I was grateful to him —it surprised me to note the stubborn expression that came into the nurse's eyes and the reluctance with which she went out. Even in the open door she stopped, made a silly excuse about Max returning at any minute, and compounded this by saying that Dr. Brandt knew more about sickroom diets than she did— a palpable lie.

In the end, though, she went. I turned to Scotty, more nervous than ever at the long delay in getting through this painful revelation. I blurted out, "I can hear!"

I expected astonishment, pleasure, shock—almost

anything but Scotty's wise blue eyes calmly, quietly
studying me and the serene prompting of his voice.
"Yes, I know. For how long?"

I stumbled on, hypnotized by that serenity. "Since I
woke up about half an hour ago. No—longer, I think.
I heard—"

"A moment." He got up and went over to the hall
door. Nurse Tusingham had left it ajar, and he looked
out in the hall, both ways, then closed the door, came
across the room, and motioned me to sit down beside
him in the chair vacated by Constable Wattersley.
"Keep your voice very low and tell me. I knew there
was something. I've watched you since you came into
the room. There was a difference about you, an alertness. Even Max noticed it, I'm sure. It was as though
you held yourself stiff, and so as not to betray anything."

"It's true. I was terrified." He was so understanding,
as he had been from our first meeting at the hotel in
Richmond, that I felt an enormous burden shifted from
me to his broad and capable shoulders. I leaned forward in my chair and tried to put all my persuasive
powers to work. "Scotty, listen to me. I've thought and
thought about that conversation I overheard at the
stationer's. And strictly speaking, Mr. Putney started it
all. I mean . . ."

Scotty smiled; yet somehow, I felt he would not be
easy to convince. "You mean our murderer fired in
self-defense?"

I agreed eagerly. "Well, he did! In a way. It really
was in defense of his life."

"My dear girl, that is no concern of yours or mine,
is it? It depends entirely upon the jury. I have a feeling
you are about to tell me something unpleasant—about
someone . . . we like."

"Oh yes. Yes! And I'm sure there are extenuating
circumstances. He wouldn't deliberately hurt anyone.
He helps people. Guns and things like that, they're not

like him. Actually, I've never seen him with a gun or
. . . any murderous weapon like that."

Scotty ran his hand over his face and repeated
thoughtfully, "He helps people. . . . He is obviously
someone here, and since you have recognized his voice,
it must be someone you have seen in the past half hour.
. . . But my dear girl, Max Brandt has used guns since
he was ten. He is never without one."

After the first shock of that, I said furiously, "I don't
believe you. He's been good to me. Saved my life. And
I paid him back by selling him out. We must *do* something. Can't I testify in his favor?"

Scotty got up, ruffling his hair until it stood on end.
In other circumstances this would have made me smile.
He looked much more inadequate than I knew him to
be. He walked over to the door and then appeared to
have a change of heart. "Am I to understand you are
willing to swear to the identity of the voice you heard
in the Putney shop?"

"Yes, but that is not conclusive, after all. They
would need a great deal more evidence, wouldn't they?
Someone to prove motive. That sort of thing."

In a stern voice that frightened me, Scotty said,
"Once Max Brandt's name is mentioned in connection
with the Putney death, it may not be difficult to discover a motive and the rest. Listen to me, Nona." He
took me by the shoulder and shook me a little. I was
sure he thought he was shaking sense into me. "Putney
was a part of a conspiracy by a foreign power. You
know something of this already. I needn't go into the
details. The constable tonight rather foolishly told too
much about things that have been going on, even in his
jurisdiction. But as to Max—if he was the man you
heard. From your testimony about their conversation,
his and Putney's, we think Putney was trying to with-
draw from this crowd when he was silenced by the man
you heard. The executioner."

"No. Not Max! He's one of you. Not an enemy."

"He was born an enemy. We used him because we

believed he'd come over to us. But he's always had a grievance against us. We knew that. It was a question of whether he'd gotten over it or not. Apparently, he never has. You see, although he'd come over to us during the war and was a liaison with our men on the Continent, his wife never had. She was a dedicated Communist. Shortly after the end of the war, she was shot in a raid on a terrorist headquarters in a little town on the Rhine. We thought Max was with us in spite of this. But . . . you see? He's never really forgiven us."

"You trusted him before. He's never betrayed you yet, has he?"

Scotty shrugged. "How can we know? He may be the answer to several riddles we've never solved. He spent years in Yorkshire after the war, helping us with his knowledge of workings behind the Curtain. But sometimes they do that. They play their part for years. They are perfectionists. And if Max has been betraying us all these years, then I hope . . . No matter." He stopped, seeing in my face the horror I felt, which must have shown in my eyes. "Fair play, and all that. Word of honor."

I couldn't speak, to thank him, but he understood and nodded to me as he went out into the dark, creaking little hall.

So it was Ilona, Max Brandt's wife, who had motivated his treachery all these years! That would explain the bitterness I had noticed so often in him, and it wasn't as though Max had kept his wife's memory secret from me. Upon several occasions, as I thought back now, her name had come up. He had even called me "Ilona." He said he had saved me because I looked like his dead wife, who was . . . "executed."

That made his treason and his guilt suddenly very clear. Small wonder that Dr. Max Brandt had been the first on the scene of the Putney murder and been able to rescue me—since he needed only to come hurrying through the shop after killing the man, to find me lying

there unconscious in the doorway. He might even have stumbled over my body. How careless of me to have delayed his escape!

I went to the open door after Scotty left, feeling horribly alone and desolate. I did not care for Scotty as I had loved Max, but he was such a comfort to have around that I missed his presence. At the same time, my heart twisted with pain and also in relief when I heard Nurse Tusingham call out to Scotty, who was going down the noisy front stairs, "They've not seen Doctor in the kitchen. What do you make of it?"

"Be quiet!" Scotty's voice called sharply, and I thought his deliberate footsteps increased their pace.

I went out to the head of the stairs and listened, hoping against hope that they would not find Max. The detestable nurse's voice came and went, as though she might be prowling around, checking Max's whereabouts.

"The Humber lad's out here. He thinks he saw Doctor running toward the back a minute ago."

I rushed back through the hall, stopping just a few seconds to push aside the dusty drapes in the parlor. The parlor overlooked the front of the hotel, and all I could see was the empty street full of shadows, with an occasional passerby. Max might be anywhere among those shadows, desperate to escape, hounded because I had had the appalling luck to walk into Mr. Putney's shop at that time, out of all the other minutes in the world.

Scotty's car was parked in front of the hotel, and a small shadow moved beside it. I looked out more closely. The curious radiance formed by the moon upon the low ground fog illuminated the face of the shadowy figure, and I saw Tod Humber's friendly, mischievous, freckled face. He looked more mischievous than ever, and I wondered what he was up to.

There was no betraying creak of the floorboards behind me; yet I suddenly knew that I was not alone. I turned, hesitating because the only person I wanted

was outside somewhere, running or hiding, gone from my life until we would meet one terrible day in some courtroom, where my words must destroy him a second time. If I could see him just once more, to tell him how sorry I was and—yes, I admitted it to myself—try to find out if he had ever really loved me at all or if it had always been only my resemblance to his dead wife.

But when I looked around, Max Brandt was standing close behind me, one hand out tentatively, as if pleading with me, while his dark face, unreadable, looked at me.

It was I who pleaded, after all. "I had to tell Scotty. You must have always known I would have to find out. It didn't change my feelings . . . only yours. Do you hate me now?"

"Nona, come with me." His voice was quiet, hardly more than a whisper, but I did not miss a syllable. He added with just a hint of his old authority, "Now, *Liebchen*. We've no time."

"Where to?" I asked, to give myself a moment's delay while I prayed for some hint that I should obey him.

Before he answered, he kissed me as in the better days, gently, on the cheek. At the same time something snapped hard against the window behind us. I jumped nervously.

"A pebble," Max said. "The boy's signal to us." He opened the bedroom door, picked up my shoes, and threw them to me. In something of a trance I stepped into them, and he hurried me along to the hall.

"Where are we going?" I repeated.

He did not stop as he told me in that low, resonant voice which made me fear Scotty so near us and liable to overhear. "Where you want me to go. Back to London. If I can get you safely there before *they* find out, you'll be safe there now."

"But you! They'll arrest you."

He smiled that familiar, twisted smile. "That, you will admit, was inevitable."

"Please—be careful. Scotty will hear you," I whispered, but he shook his head and pointed to Tod Humber, who was leaping into the tiny reception hall below the stairs.

As the boy ran toward the back of the hotel and I assumed, toward the kitchen, he yelled loudly, "Out the back, Inspector. By the pantry, he was."

Max took my arm, and we hurried down the stairs, out the front door that Tod had left open, and into the foggy street, still luminous in patches where the moon pierced the fog. Max's little red MG was where we had left it early in the day when Constable Wattersley forced us to return. As we reached the car, I asked him, "Wouldn't it be better if you went back with Scotty? This way, you will only antagonize him." Then I remembered the Humbers and the rest of it. "He doesn't believe me about them, and I suppose now he'd never believe you, would he?"

"Oh no," Max laughed harshly. "He wouldn't believe me now. I've got to give myself over. And in any case, we've got that gang of simple-minded peasant spies to watch out for. Scotty and that idiot constable put great faith in them, I assure you."

He got in beside me and started the car while I was still staring at him. "Max! Have you thought! Would I have to testify against you?"

"You will tell exactly what you heard and no more. No less."

I nodded to Max and touched his hand, knowing he would understand that I believed him. His fingers closed on mine. Then he drove across from the end of the street into the dusty trail over the downs.

"We should cut off some distance this way."

I knew we would cross into the highway near the Humber Inn, and as we bumped along through the fog-shrouded heath, I asked, "Wouldn't it be quicker by the road?"

"Yes, but Altmann is there."

"Who is that?"

"He came down from London. He is one of *them*."

I remembered the square-faced, sinister blond man and his blond, silent woman. "I know him. A friend of Humber's. A nasty-looking German."

He slapped the wheel around to avoid a chalky boulder and glanced at me momentarily. "I too am a nasty-looking German."

I had forgotten. I said suddenly, "Did you really love me when you offered to marry me and took me so far?"

"I did. I do." He looked at my face and smiled, this time with a wistfulness that was new and sat strangely but wonderfully upon his hard features. "Not very romantic, is it? Not like your girlhood dreams; yet there are no words that say it more directly." He went on speaking as he peered through the radiant white fog that disguised everything into thousands of unnatural shapes. "You see, I knew all along that you must hear again. I wanted to tell you myself, but there wasn't time. There never was time. I wanted you to be safe when I told you."

"Couldn't you have told me in Richmond, if my real danger was only from the mur—from you?"

"Do you think that? My dear child, do you really think Putney's killer is the only danger threatening you? What of the rest of them?"

"I know. Scotty told me. He says the constable doesn't know enough about his own area."

Womanlike, I had been most troubled, not by my possible danger from Max, but by the idea that Scotty may have been right. Max really loved only one woman, the dead Ilona. But the question was hard to approach.

I ventured first on another but smaller complaint. "I thought tonight, when you said you were going to get my supper, that you'd deserted me again, as you did at the Humber Inn."

"I did not desert you at the inn, Nona. And I would not have deserted you at Combe Coster." He touched his jaw, and I glanced at the ugly bruise there. "Your Humber friends knocked me out last evening when I went down to investigate. It wasn't until I started to prowl around there after I'd left you in the room that I realized they were all part of the thing I was trying to get you away from. By then, it was too late. Humber, or that blond fellow, Altmann, knocked me out, and I came to consciousness behind the wheel of my car just off the road, halfway to Combe Coster. You may imagine how frantic I was when I found you'd disappeared from the inn with the Humber lad."

"But today, when you met Scotty in his car out on the downs, why didn't you tell him? He still believes in those people."

I thought of something else too, but it was so horrible that I refused to acknowledge it. Max had been out there on the downs, and alone, before he met Scotty. Had Max been my attacker today? No! Never!

Max said nothing to my mention of the downs, possibly because the moon, gleaming in that odd way through the fog, played such tricks upon our eyes, changing shapes of rocks and rolling hills. He was staring ahead intently.

"What is it?" I asked nervously.

"I don't know. They may not have tried to take the car after all. Tod said he was going to tamper with Scotty's car to prevent its starting, but they may have taken the footpath over the downs to cut us off."

Before I could make any betraying sound, I stuffed my knuckles into my mouth. Max was right. Eerie shadows seemed to grow long and then to shrivel across the trail in front of us, just beyond a series of hillocks covered by bushy shrubs. There were a number of these shapes that caught a kind of nimbus made up of moon and fog. At first, it was impossible to see what they could be, but nothing would have frightened me more than the sight I caught now ahead of us in the

road, of many shadows and, most prominently to me, the tall, uniformed Nurse Tusingham, her stiff head-dress gleaming so that she looked like a standing figure on a Pharaoh's tomb, and as unreal. The moon gleamed horribly on bits of her face, and especially her big, serviceable teeth, as she grinned at us in the head-lights of Max's car.

Chapter Eighteen

ABRUPTLY, Max jerked the wheel so that we bumped
along the edge of a little embankment and passed the
eerie figure of the nurse with several feet to spare. I
saw other luminous creatures rush along the trail behind her. The MG skidded past them, avoiding them
by inches.

I cried out to Max, "Stop! I see Scotty." It would
double Max's danger at his trial if he deliberately
flouted the law in the person of Inspector MacLeish.

Whether he heard me or not, he seemed to speed
up, and I had to hold on hard, praying for a safe, clear
road ahead. Almost at once there was a sound like an
explosion, and the rear-view mirror spattered broken
glass over us. I think Max would have raced on, for he
pushed me down hard to keep me out of range of the
gunshots, but I screamed at him to stop, and thrust my
foot out hard, bringing my heel down on his instep.
Another shot missed us altogether, but my foot had
done more damage. The car ripped up bushes and
came to a jarring halt, tilted at a twenty-degree-angle
against a big stone marker.

Max put his arm out in front of me, as I was
plunged forward, and barely saved me from diving into
the windscreen. He said in a furious voice in which
there was desperation, "Run! Never mind what happens here. Run!"

Confused by this, and shaken by the accident to the
car, I stumbled when the car door swung open. But for
Max's quick hand behind me, I would have gone down
on my knees. As it was, there came one breathtaking
second when I could have followed his astonishing ad-

vice and run, leaving Max to fend them off. I did not run, because Scotty was coming toward me in great, purposeful strides.

He took my reluctant hand, saying quietly, "It's no use, you know. You'd have done better to rely upon me. I might be able to help Max in some way."

The man who had fired the shots was Jolyon Humber, and he still had the heavy handgun that looked a little like a pistol when he came up to Max on the other side of the MG. Max looked dark and furious and—to me, at least—dangerous. I was sure Max would be violent. I only hoped the trouble he caused would not destroy him. If only he and I had been permitted to reach London so that he might surrender himself without Scotty's interference!

"You disappoint me, Nona," said Scotty in his pleasant way. In other circumstances that tolerant air of his would have shamed me, but now I was nearly as furious as Max. I could not see what Max was doing when approached by Humber, but I had my first tiny surge of relief when I saw that Tod Humber was lingering along on the outskirts of the eerie little group.

And an eerie group it was! The blond Altmann and his silent lady friend, the pretty Pam, and above all, Nurse Tusingham, began to close in upon our group. With the fog winding around us in great puffs, the moonlight was able to coat only their heads, so that these monsters all appeared to have halos.

I stood my ground fiercely before Scotty, who was trying to herd me along toward what he supposed were his friends. I tried to tell him in a low voice, "Don't you understand, Scotty? One of those people tried to strangle me today out on the Stones. They are all in it together. That's why I couldn't count on them to help you with Max. They would kill him—and me, too!"

"My dear Nona, that gun the good Humber is waving so melodramatically is Max Brandt's own Luger. Max is the only one here who uses such weapons as a general thing. Who knows better than you? Putney was

killed with an old-fashioned Luger. Come now. Do behave. We are going to drive back to London. You can
have no objection to that. You would have gone—or
thought you would go—with Brandt."

"Max *is* going to surrender in London," I said, trying
to see around Scotty and the others to Max, but Jol
Humber was still waving the gun that Scotty said had
belonged to Max, and that, combined with the little red
MG, kept me from seeing Max. Everyone seemed to be
talking except Tod Humber and me. I thought I heard
Max call out to me, but I could not understand him.
And then, the fog shrouded him and Humber and that
awful gun. I wondered if Humber had kept that gun
since he and his friends knocked Max out last night.
Scotty was being incredibly stupid about these creatures.

Along the road toward me at the same minute
stalked Nurse Tusingham, and I drew away from her,
revolted as always at her presence.

Scotty took my arm firmly. "Come now. She won't
hurt you. She and Humber are here to see after Max.
You needn't worry. She won't trouble you. Get about it,
Bertha. Max doesn't like it. Not the least."

"Aye, aye, sir," the woman mocked, and stalked
away.

"Where are we going?" I asked, tired, sick, caring
for very little except that Max should get to London
and give himself up of his own volition, because anything else would be disastrous to his chances.

Scotty said, "We are going to Humber's car. And
then to London. That was what you intended, wasn't
it?"

"With Max. Yes."

Scotty was moving along with me at a surprisingly
slow pace. He looked at me now like a schoolteacher
whose pupil disappoints him. "Nona, you are being very
silly. Forget this girlish, giggling attraction and consider what you have done. You have harbored a man

you confess you know to be a criminal. Have you thought of that?"

"Many times," I said, but I was walking on tiptoe, trying to catch a glimpse of Max, who must be there in that luminous fog, at the mercy of the hideous Jolyon Humber and that ugly gun.

When Scotty saw my glance he shook his head. "Humber is a good man. He won't make any mistakes."

I could not understand it. As I stumbled over a ridge of dirt in the path, my heel turning over, I stopped to test my heel, but I was worrying over something quite different. I could not make out Max and his bodyguard now at all, but there were still the weird, half-visible creatures around us. Tod, who had said nothing to me, kept trying to catch my eye, while I angrily avoided him, feeling he had betrayed both Max and me. The blond man, Altmann, and his female comrade had slowed and were behind Scotty and me now, finding it difficult to keep such a slow pace as I gave them.

I had a strange, sudden notion that Scotty was slowing so that something might be done. I did not know what that might be, and the only thing that kept me clinging to my last trust in him was the knowledge that when I called London this morning, he had been known at Scotland Yard, or at least, among the police and detective divisions we reached when we asked for Scotland Yard.

I spoke very softly, careful to avoid being heard by any one of the others. "Scotty, you act as if this Humber gang can be trusted. Believe me, you may think what you like about my reasons, but Jolyon Humber and that yellow-haired man murdered a man named Leecher."

Scotty did not seem surprised, though his frank, wide eyes narrowed a trifle. "Aren't you forgetting? Several persons are of the impression that you yourself knocked Leecher off the Stones."

"But why would I do that, for heaven's sake?"

"To prevent his reporting your whereabouts to Scotland Yard, of course."

"Was he really with Scotland Yard? I didn't know," I lied, adding stiffly, "You may not believe me, but I had nothing to do with that man."

He grinned. "No. Don't trouble to deny it. I didn't take the accusation seriously. I merely remind you of it so that you will see how damaging accusations like yours can be. Jolyon Humber has not actually committed any crime that you can prove—has he?"

It was a confusing point. I was so tired and so worried about Max that for a minute I really couldn't answer him. Then, as we tramped up over one of those little hills which seemed endless because they were so like all the others, I remembered.

"Humber and these others searched my room. They knocked Max unconscious. They would have killed me. Why they didn't kill Max, I don't know. But one of them was still after me today."

Scotty glanced off to the north, toward the Stones and the place where he and Max had met me in that old beat-up car.

"I remember. It had something to do with the sheet and the rope I found. The sheet was off the bed at the Humber Inn where you rested yesterday afternoon."

"You can't seriously think I carried that sheet around with me all last night, in order to pretend to use it today!"

He shrugged in a way that suggested anything was possible.

"It had to be someone close by," I said. "I saw your car just seconds before I was attacked. Max said you and he met just about there in that little gulley where I saw your car. Then that means . . ."

Scotty was watching me thoughtfully. "I see what you mean. Max Brandt was there alone, close enough to have made the attack."

"He is fond of me. Why would he try to kill me?"

"To prevent your recovery and your testimony

against him. Naturally. Has it occurred to you that Max may have intended to kill you sometime in that ride you supposed was to be in the direction of London tonight?"

"No. It hasn't!" I scuffed over the chalky ground, so carried away by a sudden, astonishing realization that I almost said it aloud. I only thought it, after all, but it was impossible to keep the idea from showing in my face, and I turned away.

If Max was alone and close enough to have attacked me out there, the same thing applied to Scotty. The difference was that I had believed, because the car was there, that Scotty was in the car. That need not follow, at all. Scotty, quite as easily as Max, might have attacked me. The horror of this was extremely difficult to conceal. But the insanity of suspecting Detective Inspector MacLeish of Scotland Yard was borne upon me even as I considered it, and I knew there must be another explanation, some strange reason why all these people behaved so oddly.

"Where is Max now?" I asked, trying to see into the radiant white dark where Max and Nurse Tusingham had disappeared. "Couldn't we hurry a little faster? Then we could return to London together. If you were present, Max wouldn't make any move to—"

Across the little hills there were sounds, muffled but very like scuffling, then a faint cry that wavered through the shimmering night. I swung around.

Scotty reached for me, gently but with firmness. "Steady, old girl. You'll slip."

Cutting harshly into the sound of his voice was a shot, a terrible noise that seemed to explode in the tight, thick air around us. I screamed and tried to rush down the little hill toward the trail, but I couldn't free myself from Scotty's grasp. I twisted and turned my wrist, but his fingers cut into them, much harder, stronger, more brutal than I had ever known him to be.

"It's Max! Humber's shot him!" I cried. "Let me go. Scotty! Let me go to him."

I was still struggling, thrusting out and kicking at

him as viciously as I could, when a big figure materialized, ever so faintly, out of that luminous fog. I prayed, *Let it be Max. Oh, please, please, let it be Max.* . . .

But the stiffened coil of Nurse Tusingham loomed up vaguely and beside her, lumbering forward, a little hesitant, as if uncertain of his reception from Scotty, was Jolyon Humber. He mumbled something, which I drowned by my scream at him.

"Murderer! Murderer! Now you see, Scotty. Now you know what he really is."

And then, as I looked at Scotty, waiting for him to rage at the cowardly act of Humber, I remembered that dreadful suspicion which had come to me a few minutes before, a suspicion so long in coming because it was so incredible.

"You know what Humber was. And the others. You wanted Humber to do this! You planned it the minute you got here."

"My dear girl, don't be so naïve. Jol! Is it over?"

"Over, sir. He—he was shot while escaping."

Humber looked shaken. The gun was in his hand, and he looked at it as if it were a strange new toy.

Scotty corrected him crisply, very official. "Please, Jol, not quite so Yankee. The German spy, Brandt, wanted for questioning in the matter of three murders, was shot while eluding these good citizens."

"Three murders!" I repeated, so shocked that I forgot my fear of them all. "You'll never prove such a thing. Without my testimony you couldn't even prove one murder!"

Nurse Tusingham stalked across the road and toward us on our little hill. "You're free to get about it, Scotty. I'll manage you, dearie. These things are quite painless, they do say." She laughed, a crunching, hideous noise as she came up to tower over me. She reached for me, and when I tried wildly to kick at her, she was too clever, getting between me and the others, blotting me from their sight.

Scotty took several steps down the hill and held out his hands. Jolyon Humber moved forward, his figure half-concealed by fog, only his teeth and eyes and the hand with the gun shining in the reflected radiance of the moon. He tossed the gun to Scotty, who turned and looked up the little rise toward me. I couldn't see the others now, nor had I seen them in the last few terrible minutes, not the Altmanns or Pam Wattersley, or even Tod. We seemed to be alone in this dead world, just Humber and Scotty, the nurse and me. I knew then why we were alone. There were to be only the essential witnesses to this murder, and I still did not know the "why" of anything.

"Nona," Scotty called to me gently. "You had better run."

I knew then why Scotty had taken the heavy German gun from Humber. I was to be Max's third "murder victim." In a kind of nightmare, I heard him and understood. If I did run I would never get twenty yards away; yet so desperately did I cling to life and the one faint chance that Max was only wounded and could still be saved, that I scrambled to get away from Nurse Tusingham. Unaccountably, the woman held on, her big shadow falling between me and Scotty.

Scotty raised the gun. With a great twist at the nurse's forearm, I released myself and spun around, to plunge down behind the hill into the glistening dark. There was a curious metallic sound behind me. Nurse Tusingham had moved abruptly, confusing me as much by her erratic behavior as by Scotty's puzzled stare at that gun in his hand which was pointed at me.

Behind him, where Humber stood, a voice called to him through the fog, and for an instant I wondered how Humber could sound so much like the dearest voice in the world to me, that of Max Brandt. Scotty was as staggered as I.

"It's no use, Scotty. You heard the last shot from that little beauty."

Humber jumped nervously and scuttled across the rutted trail that separated him from Scotty, who turned at his approach, still holding the big Luger that momentarily seemed to threaten Humber. But these two men had ceased to interest me when I realized that the voice out of the rolling white fog was actually real.

I cried out as loudly as I could across the weird, unworldly atmosphere that still separated us, "Max! Max! Are you there? Are you all right?"

"Stay where you are, Nona. Don't move."

I remained rigid, only half-understanding what had happened in these last few seconds but wildly grateful to Fate, to God, to whatever accident or purpose had prevented Humber from succeeding as Scotty's instrument of death. I was aware, however, of the long shadow that hovered over me, and I wondered if Max was aware of the real and final danger, the menace of his old subordinate Bertha Tusingham.

Scotty managed to retain a calm I could not help admiring. "You have a way of forgetting essentials, Brandt. That is why you were of such little service to the Party. Look up there. The lady who betrayed you and was so sorry, so terribly sorry! See who is guarding her. Your old friend Bertha. I suggest you behave sensibly and give Humber the weapon you have—as I suppose you do have one. And this time, make it the weapon that works. Not like this nasty trick of yours with the Luger."

I deliberately did not glance to my left. I knew the monolithic figure of Nurse Tusingham was there, undoubtedly staring at me, reaching out one of those strong hands, awaiting only the order from Scotty—who called to her now.

"Closer, Bertha. Show him that we are no longer playing our little game. This business ends tonight."

The woman touched me. I could feel her hand as it reached out, and when I shifted a trifle to avoid her, Scotty yelled, "Put your gun to her head. If Brandt takes another step, shoot."

Chapter Nineteen

I TRIED to see Max more clearly. I wanted to be sure he was there, very much alive, not some desperately conjured dream of mine in this moment which might be my last. He had moved closer behind Humber, and Scotty had to turn a trifle to keep a close watch on Max as well as the nurse and me.

Max spoke in a little more than his ordinary voice; yet we all heard him, all of us in this little point of light out of the enormous dark around us. "Your game has been up for a long time, MacLeish. By all means, give your orders. Ask Tusey to shoot."

I hardly knew the full implication of that, for Scotty called immediately to Nurse Tusingham, "It won't be quite as neat as it might have been with his weapon, but that idiot constable and his oafish villagers will hardly find any difference."

I stood perfectly straight, as Max had asked me to do. I felt the cold touch of something against my temple, and after a second of suspense very like death to me, I knew the cold touch was the nurse's forefinger, not the weapon I feared.

"Fire!" cried Scotty, staring first at us, and then around at the stupefied Humber and at Max, whose face had one of those humorless smiles which I had come to know so well. Max shook his head as Scotty's hand went into the breast of his macintosh.

"It's too late. The cozy little Party cell is gone. And don't be a fool at this late date. Constable Wattersley and his men have you in their sights."

I think I was as amazed as Scotty when the stout little constable, in his quaint uniform and helmet,

gradually emerged from the white layers of fog with Tod Humber, sober and unhappy, hurrying beside him. There were other heads, other bodies, now gradually illuminated in a ghostly circle around us. They appeared to be villagers, and I knew they must 'have heard Scotty's cruel, cutting dismissal of their ability, for they looked as grim as the Stones on the distant horizon.

"Bertha!" Scotty cried again. "We've got our hostage. Shoot!"

"Can't hardly do that, sir, begging pardon," said Nurse Tusingham. "Seeing that the doctor's got my gun."

"How . . . when . . . ?" His last card played, Scotty swung around toward Humber, suddenly very white, his blue eyes blazing.

"Ay. It's true enough." Humber nodded, cowering under Scotty's look. "She'll be . . . a real Yarder, that nurse. She's with the police, that one."

I could hardly believe what he said, and as the constable and the others moved forward, enclosing Scotty and Humber in a wall of silence, I felt the sinister quality of the villagers' resentment. Then I noticed the dreaded touch of the woman at my side. She patted me on the back.

"Good girl, dearie! You did just right, doing as doctor said. It will go a long way toward doctor's trial, him and you playing bold as brass like you did."

I only half-believed the poor woman. Nor was I interested in her. Max was hurrying over the intervening space between us. He seized me, lifting me entirely off the ground as we embraced.

"My poor darling . . . my poor *Liebchen*," he kept whispering, and kissed me again. I said nothing. I was too busily engaged in hugging and kissing him.

It was many hours before I could stop believing that someone was liable to murder me if I closed my eyes or that at any minute I might be the target of some faceless assassin who had "murdered" the stationer.

That Dear Constable Wattersley, whom I, along with Scotty MacLeish, had so much underestimated, "took in charge" Scotty and Humber as he had taken the Altmanns and his own sister, the beautiful Pam. I did not want to know what happened to them, or what would happen when they had their trial and I was forced to testify.

I was happy to be near Max, to know there was hope for him and, selfishly, that there was hope for the two of us together. It was too much to take in before I rested that night—both the joys that might come and the horrors we had escaped would have to wait. And when Nurse Tusinghim told me, as she tucked me in, that the real CID man protecting me had been Alfred Skipton and not the bogus Inspector MacLeish, I couldn't even remember who the little man was. Which was a pity, for I recalled later, when I awoke, how very active that man had been in following Max and me everywhere and asking me his jolly little questions in that casual way.

I was still tired the next morning, and I'm sure even Max felt the same letdown of all the physical energies that had taken him this far in the company of a woman who might, at any minute, recover her hearing and destroy him by that hearing. Nevertheless, when I awoke shortly after nine, aching in every muscle and every bone, there was Max and my nemesis, Nurse Tusingham, leaning over the bed almost as I remembered them those first days of silence.

Max kissed me gently, then studying my face, looked me over in a professional way. "Do you feel well enough to travel, Nona?"

"Where to?"

"Tussey and I want to drive up to London and get this thing settled as soon as possible. I don't like to go without you. I was so close to losing you. Darling, how do you feel, honestly?"

"I'm quite all right." I sat up at once, delighted that Max wanted me. We held each other's hands as I asked

Nurse Tusingham uneasily, "Will it go badly with Max? I don't understand anything. Are you really a detective, Miss Tusingham?"

"Call me Tussey. No, I'm not a Detective Inspector, dearie. Nothing so grand. I'm in the right field when I'm doctor's nurse here. But I'm sent out on special cases, as you might say." She grinned, that big grin which had heretofore set me to shivering. "And when Doctor Brandt came in some two years ago and more, and told us what he knew about your friend Scotty's Party cell, instead of arresting Max for his part in it, my—er—employers played the innocent, made Max cross as sticks by denying he'd told 'em anything of importance, and I popped up as a dear old Red-celling Party member. See? All simple as that!"

I understood vaguely that Miss Tusingham was a spy planted by the government in a nest of enemy agents, but thus far I had learned nothing about the head and brains of *them,* the strange man who had been known to me as Detective Inspector Scotty MacLeish. All else I could believe—that from the beginning he had masterminded the attacks on me, the only witness to a murder committed by a member of his cell. But I was still unable to reconcile my calls to London and my firm belief in his identity with the true story, which Max and Tussey told me as we drove up to London from Combe Coster that day.

"I suppose all this is very hush-hush," I said, sitting a trifle cramped but very safe, crushed between Max and Nurse Tusingham in the front seat.

"Oh, frightfully," Tussey agreed, "but she is entitled to have it unraveled—don't you think, Max, old boy?"

"She should know one thing above all," said Max, looking at me in such a dear way that I did not have the heart to remind him that we were driving at considerable speed on a very narrow, curving road and that he should keep an eye on that road. "She should know that I did kill Putney and that, in a sense, it was murder. Do you remember, Nona, when Scotty told you

I worked with Scotland Yard on certain matters? It is perfectly true, except that Scotty was not what he claimed to be. And he certainly did not know I was exactly what he claimed for me."

I remembered very well. Everything about that plain, pleasant, ordinary Scotty MacLeish puzzled me. "I remember that, Max, but I called London yesterday. They said Inspector MacLeish was out."

The nurse laughed. I tried not to dislike that laugh as much as I had. "Of course. Scotty never did things by halves. And the funny thing is, though they've never met, the real Detective Inspector MacLeish looks a little like him, wouldn't you say, Max? That was just an example of Scotty's thoroughness. The truth is, Scotty only expected to use the alias for one visit to you. To be quite sure Max and I were telling him the truth when we said you couldn't identify one of Scotty's men—Max —as the murderer. We groaned, I tell you, girl, with fear that you'd blurt out something to make him act before we could protect you. But there was no other way. Scotty was a slippery customer, as the Yanks say. We couldn't have him taken in charge merely because of something we suspected he might do."

Terribly puzzled, I murmured, "Please tell it from the beginning."

"Good God, no!" Max exclaimed. "That would be going back as far as poor Ilona. My wife—my first wife," he put in with a smile at me. "In the Underground during the war, in Berlin and Dresden, she was violently Communist. I tried to get her to see things, but in short, she was killed in a raid on a terrorist cell some years ago. I was bitter. I fell into the opposite trap. I took over Ilona's work. I was planted in England, in the north. It was petty work, disgusting, and it interfered with my real profession. I reported the whole thing to Scotland Yard, and they did nothing. Or so I thought."

"That was where I came on, and a very good thing I made of it, if I do say," Nurse Tusingham inter-

rupted. "I was assigned to old Max. 'Stick like a plaster,' they told me. And I did. Got myself into Scotty's messy business, and Scotty himself attached me to Max.

I began to see dim light in the evil that had surrounded me. "Then Mr. Putney found out about you, Max, and pulled the gun—I saw that, Max! I'm witness to it. He did pull a gun. And you shot him in self-defense."

"Optimist," said Max. "At any rate, you are nearly right. I did not immediately confess to Scotland Yard about that act, which is what gives me the difficulty now. In any case, when Putney and I exchanged those disastrous shots, I found you in the doorway. Scotty came. He had been intending to meet Putney, one of the cell. The truth of it is, he wanted you dead. I didn't. When I told him you couldn't hear and might not have recognized me, he and one of *them* made that little visit to you, as Scotland Yard men. After, he had to keep up the role, at least until he'd had you murdered in some safe way. Safe for the cell, that is to say. Poor Leecher—who really was an inspector—and Tussy decided they couldn't wait. They had to get you to safety in London."

"And I ran away from them. From you, Miss Tusingham! When you might have saved me all this."

"Well, is that all the thanks I am to get?" Max demanded. "How was I to know the police still did not trust me? In any case, I'd already decided I was going to get Nona out of reach of Scotty until, at least, she could recover."

"Even at the price of promising to marry me," I said severely.

"Certainly. No sacrifice was too great. But I made my biggest mistake when I stopped at Humber's Inn. I've known Jol slightly for years, but for some idiotic reason, I did not know he was in it with Scotty. He called in this Altmann. . . ." He looked over at the nurse. "Do you think we will ever know how they found out Leecher?"

There were papers on him mentioning me," I said.
"Tod and I found them. Humber and Altmann had
killed him. We saw the two men returning from the
Stones. And Leecher was on that ledge Tod calls his
cave. They must have killed him. Hit him probably
and then knocked him off the Stones. How else can we
explain that they were coming from there when we saw
them, and they made no report of Leecher's body?"

"I know," Max agreed. "The boy reported very much
as you have. He will be needed in London as well, poor
devil."

We rode in silence for a little while, each of us with
some horror to remember, Max and I with the warm
knowledge of each other's feelings, the tenderness, and
now the understanding.

He must have guessed what I was thinking, for he
said suddenly, "Nona, you knew why I had to go
through that business last night, when I found you
could hear. I had to take Scotty's attention from you.
When Bertha arrived, I knew we had a secret ally.
Bertha tried to keep Scotty occupied. Young Tod
helped her, but as you know, Scotty came after us anyway."

I knew I would never forget that wild ride across
the downs and its nightmarish climax last night. "Don't
I said quickly. "Let's talk about something else. Like
how very odd it is that Scotty, who made such a con-
vincing Detective Inspector, should waste his life being
an enemy agent."

Tussey laughed, but Max didn't. I think he agreed
with me. We were just passing the Humber Inn, which
gave me the shivers, and I was surprised when Max
stopped. But when Tod Humber came out carrying a
battered, old-fashioned man's valise, I understood.

"I thought we could take the boy up with us," Max
explained. "Poor little devil feels like a Judas."

And besides, I thought, *Tod has no one now.* I
wanted to show Max I understood his unspoken kindness. I kissed him lightly on the cheek.

He turned and said in that very special and tender voice, "Thank you, *Liebchen.*"

Tod came over. We all greeted him, and he blurted out, "I had to do it. I didn't want to call Constable last night and put Uncle to prison. But I had to."

"We are not to think of such things now," Max told him, smiling a little. "We are all under orders to be very gay and pleasant."

Tod grinned and seemed to feel ever so much better. He was laughing by the time we were on the road again.

"Nona, you had better send for your mother and father," Max said presently.

When I looked at Max, Tod put in from behind us, "Oh, that'll be jolly. Ever so! The Irish are such funny folk. And I'll show them all about London."

We laughed at the notion of Tod's showing my folks around a city he'd never seen before, and under cover of that laughter Max explained to me, "We don't know how this affair will end for me. But if it goes well, I want to marry you—if you still love me," he added, looking a bit unsure of me.

"What a silly question!" I said, with all my heart in the flippant words, and touched his hand nearest me.

We drove on across green, spring-touched England, and gradually the sharing of our fears and ancient griefs made them less, and we all laughed a good deal.

Late in the day when we approached our journey's end, there was a surprising blue sky over London. The city had never looked so beautiful.

About the Author

With over 5½ million books sold, Virginia Coffman is surely one of the most popular Gothic authors today. The author of fifty-two books published in both paperback and hardcover in the United States and in Europe, Virginia Coffman has also been published in magazines and has had one of her short stories adapted to the Paris stage. Film rights have been purchased for two of her Gothic novels.

Miss Coffman was born in San Francisco and spent most of her adult life in Hollywood, first as a secretary during the Howard Hughes years at RKO and later as a script editor. She now lives in Reno, Nevada, and pursues her hobbies of reading and making yearly trips to Europe. Virginia Coffman is a continuing author for NAL. Among her titles have been *The Demon Tower*, *Mist at Darkness*, and *The Beach House*.